Wind Eyes

A Woman's Reader and Writing Source

Ann Louise Williamson, Patricia Alice Albrecht,
Naomi Louisa Mountjoy Long, Carol Cullar,
Margo LaGattuta, Shanda Hansma Blue,
Lyn Coffin, Susan Bright

Edited by Susan Bright and Margo LaGattuta

Plain View Press
P. O. 33311
Austin, TX 78764

512-441-2452
sbpvp@eden.com

1

Acknowledgments:

An Egg, **Blossom Land Review**, 1994, Ann Williamson; *Milk*, **A Few Good Women,** Silver Beach Press, 1995, Ann Williamson; *A Lenten Season*, **New Texas, '95**, North Texas University, Carol Cullar; *Border Crossing*, **El Locofoco**, Chapultapec Press, July, 1996, Carol Cullar; *Desiderata, Inexplicable Burnings*, Press of the Guadalupe, Chapbook Contest, 1992, Carol Cullar; *dies mellior, El Locofoco*, Chapultapec Press, Jan., 1996, Carol Cullar; *Eulogy In White*, **Inexplicable Burnings**, Press of the Guadalupe, Chapbook Contest, 1992, also in **RiverSedge**, VII, 1992, Special Chicano Issue, Carol Cullar; *Fire, Rain, & the Need to Act*, **Frontiers: A Journal of Women Studies,** Vol. 17, No. 1, 1996, Carol Cullar; *he's crossed the river*, **Borderlands**, vol. #4, Spring/Summer 1994, and **Texas Short Fiction**, Vol. II, 1995, Carol Cullar; *Grace*, **Sulphur River Review**, Spring, 1994, Carol Cullar; *Howie Wazatski*, **Kalliope: A Journal of Women's Art**, Spring, 1995, Carol Cullar; *last night over*, **Negative Capability**, 1996, Carol Cullar; *Peace sleep with her*, **New Texas '95**, Carol Cullar; *Relámpago*, **Voices West**, Spring 1996, Carol Cullar; *The Alaska Question*, **Chiron Review,** Fall, 1994, Carol Cullar; *The Serpent Asks*, "*Why Not?*" and *The Supplicant or The Bird Goddess Visits, Superstition, Myth & Magik*, **The MacGuffin**, June 1996, Carol Cullar; *the sound of gravid*, **New Texas '95**, Carol Cullar; *What Fat Women Know*, **Fireweed: A Feminist Quarterly of Writing, Politics, Art & Culture**, Spring 1996, (Canada,) Carol Cullar; *Pretending to be a Barn*, **Passages North,** 1989, also in **Noedgelines,** 1986, also in **PhenomeNews,** 1995, Margo LaGattuta; *Looking for Elvis in Kalamazoo*, HM Midwest Poetry Prize, also in **The Dream Givers,** 1990, Lake Shore Publishing, Margo LaGattuta; *Telling Stories*, **The Dream Givers,** 1990, Lake Shore Publishing, Margo LaGattuta; *The Dream Givers*, **The Dream Givers,** 1990, Lake Shore Publishing, Margo LaGattuta; *Fish on Shaved Ice*, **Diversion Road,** 1983, State Street Press, Margo LaGattuta; *Wearing the Jewels from Korea*, **The Bridge,** 1995, Margo LaGattuta; *Linen*, **Earth's Daughters,** 1982, also in **Resourceful Woman,** Edited by Julie Winklepleck & Shawn Brennan, 1994 Visible Ink Press, reprinted with permission of Gale Research, Inc., Margo LaGattuta; *My Welcome Home Illusion*, **Diversion Road,** 1983, State Street Press, also in **The Dream Givers,** 1990, Margo LaGattuta; *Light Support*, **The Bridge,** 1995, Margo LaGattuta; *Stopping for a Bite*, HM NFSPS, 1996, Margo LaGattuta; *The Wish Bracelet*, **The Bridge,** 1989, Margo LaGattuta, also in **The Dream Givers,** 1990, Lake Shore Publishing, Margo LaGattuta; *Bridge of Birds*, **Noedgelines,** 1986, Margo LaGattuta. *The Maple Wood*, **The Southern Indiana Review,** 1995, Shanda Hansma Blue; *Rhythm*, **The Flying Island**, 1994, also in **Confluence,** 1994, Shanda Hansma Blue; *Breathe through your nose*, and *Angle of Repose*, **The Flying Island**, 1996, Shanda Hansma Blue; *Ballet*, **The Southern Indiana Review,** 1996, Shanda Hansma Blue; *Swimming the English Channel*, **Swimming the English Channel,** by Susan Bright, 1985, Plain View Press, Austin, TX, also in a small edition by the same title from Smith/Doorstop Books, The Poetry Business Press, Huddersfield, United Kingdom, 1989; also in **Poetry Street 3**, Longram Group UK, Longram House, United Kingdom, 1990; also in **Iron,** 5 Marden Terrace, Cullercoats, North Shields, Tyne & Wear, United Kingdom, 1987.

Contents

Foreward 5
Susan Bright and Margo LaGattuta
Wind Eyes   7

I Couldn't Leave Them   11
Ann Louise Williamson

Milk   12
Little Birds   13
The Flowers the Sky   14
Relinquishing Snow   15
Baby Birds   16
The End of August   18
Green   19
A la Mode   20
As She Tosses and Turns   21
What Will Become of Us All   22
Death   23
An Opera With Dog   24
Estrogen Replacement Therapy   26
The Christ Hospital, 1961   27
November   28
An Egg   29
What the Universe Looks Like
    From Earth   30

Rose Dust   31
Patricia Alice Albrecht

Rose Dust   32
Hoola Popper   34
Skipping   38
Wing Tips   39
Just a Second Before . . .   40
Happy Happy Birthday Baby   41
Succulent   46
I Just Thought It Was Menopause
Laces   53
Blue Legs   54

Notes From My Top Pocket 57
Naomi Louisa Mountjoy Long

I am a Feather   58
So! What Nationality Are You? 59
The Untricking   60
Metamorphosis   61
Mother's Day   62
Sit Back and They Come   63
Robin   64
Unbraided   65
Out of Whack!   67
No More Skirts   68
I Really Don't Know   69
The Lawn Was Still Green   70
Driving into the Sun   71
Pacem's Memorial   72
I Hear Myself Crying   73
Poking About   74
And What's in the Drawer?   75
Recital   76
Sweet Shit   77
Driving Home   78

Hot-thighed Bride   79
Carol Cullar

Fire, Rain, and the Need to Act 80
he's crossed the river   82
Relámpago   83
The Supplicant or
    The Bird Goddess Visits   84
A Lenten Season   85
Dumb Show 86
Border Crossing   87
Desiderata   89
The Serpent Asks, "Why Not?" 90
Grace   91
Howie Wazatski   92
The Alaska Question   94
Peace Sleep with Her   95
last night over   96
What Fat Women Know   97
The Sound of Gravid   98
dies mellior   99
Eulogy In White   100

Welcome Home Illusion
101

Margo LaGattuta

Pretending to be a Barn 101
Alone in America 102
Looking for Elvis in Kalamazoo 103
Telling Stories 104
The Dream Givers 105
Briefly, in the Garden 106
Fish on Shaved Ice 107
Soft Families 108
Wearing the Jewels from Korea 110
Ultra Sounds 111
Remortgaging My House 112
Linen 113
My Welcome Home Illusion 114
On My Birthday, Bats 115
Light Support 116
Cleaning Rooms for My Mother 117
Stopping for a Bite 118
The Wish Bracelet 119
Bridge of Birds 120

Breathe Through Your Nose
121

Shanda Hansma Blue

The Maple Wood 122
On the Love of Reindeer 123
Angle of Refraction 124
Slots 126
Rhythm 127
E = MC2 128
"...ass Avenue" 130
Fall 131
Spanish Market 132
"Breathe through your nose 135
Ballet 136
Angle of Reflection 137
Maintenance 138
Angle of Repose 139
Psych 101 140

Shooting into the Light
141

Lyn Coffin

The Music Box 142
Mother's Note Home: A
    Self-Portrait 143
Chant for Nicole 145
Crystals of the Unforeseen 146
Shooting into the Light 147
Point of View Problems 156
The Psychiatrist's Second Wife 160

Hardball 169

Susan Bright

Cosmic Rabbit 169
Mother Electric 170
Axe Man 171
Wild Pitch 172
Mother Baseball 173
Double Suicide 174
Jesus Poem 175
Shoot Your Television 176
Creeps 177
Out of the Park 178
Strike Zone 179
Mother Coach 180
Jail for Kids 181
Sex With Aliens 182
Rudy Dollar 183
Swimming the English Channel 184
Myth of Proportion 189

About the Artists 190

Windows to the Soul 193
Creativity and Writing Prompts

Foreword

"Window, win'do, n. [M.E. windowe, windoge, <Scand.: cf. Icel. vindauge, window, lit. 'wind-eye'.] An opening in the wall of a building for the admission of air or light or both...."   *Living Webster, Encyclopedia of the English Language, 1977*

The story of this book is a story of community and creative process. To say it is a book created in a week is both true and misleading. The week-long publishing colony was the culmination of an eight-month process that involved selecting participants from more than three hundred entries. It is a story of logistics, travel, editing and pre-editing. It is a fact that eight women writers met at the Noisy River Publishing Colony in Ruidoso, New Mexico, from July 14-20, 1996 to create this anthology of poetry and fiction.

We didn't, for the most part, know each other. We had no idea what the book would be like. We brought families, manuscripts, computers, photographs, art and embarked on a powerful collaboration, the result of which is **Wind Eyes.** Strangers gathered that first night in the New Mexico mountain air; a community emerged.

We read to each other, found common threads in our poetry and prose. We were young, old, mothers, grandmothers, teachers, visual and theater artists. As we celebrated creative process, marveling at the way each person's voice made everyone else's work more powerful, we began to realize we were on to something important.

From a beautiful sequence of Southwestern photographs by Marty Burnett, the group chose a window, which led to the title *Wind Eyes*, when Lyn Coffin recalled from the root of the word that windows were the "eyes" of the house.

Wind Eyes became an interactive book, taking form from the process that engendered it. Each writer's section begins with an artist's statement and writing prompt. You can read and enjoy the work itself, then use it as a springboard for your own creativity. A section called "Windows to the Soul" lists more creativity and writing source ideas.

The group travelled to the prehistoric Jornado Mogollon petroglyphs at Three Rivers. There, on an outcropping of stones at the center of a wide, dry valley surrounded by mountains, we found ourselves "reading" the first books on the continent. We felt a powerful affinity to these early "writers," to their glyphs of family and clan, to the symbols of their accomplishments.

Daryl Bright Andrews literally created an ancestral photograph album, scrambling up and down the ancient granite ridge to photograph petroglyphs which had fascinated him since he was a child. Shanda Hansma Blue was drawn to the bear clan symbol, though as she recounts in the poem *Spanish Market*, her great-grandmother called her "Otter."

Wind Eyes is a celebration of family and community, of clan. Husbands, children, friends came in and out of the group, sharing music, photographs and hard work. In the natural way of women's lives, the ones we love, led and followed us through mazes that resulted in art.

John C. Andrews, co-owner of Plain View Press and Daryl Bright Andrews served as chefs, coordinators and photographers. Schuyler "Skye" Hibbard baby-sat and wrote when the computers were free. Forest William Meade Albrecht Wallenstein Miller, the youngest member was in charge of exuberance. A high point of the week occurred at his second birthday party, when he sang the alphabet perfectly—until he got to "u" and then toppled off his chair. Somewhat upset until he realized we weren't alarmed, he climbed back up and finished his letters. His father, songwriter Bruce Michael Miller, performed "There's a New Kid on the Block," — a song of love that celebrates the nurturing power of the father. How strange, we thought, for commerce to segregate parents from children, women and men from each other.

A group poem follows: a collision of intellect and art, created from a playful writing prompt. Try it with a group of friends. Each person adds a sequence of lines about a chosen topic. Without seeing what anyone else has written, fold the paper back as you pass it around a circle or scroll up on a computer screen. We dedicate our *Wind Eyes* poem to you, in honor of your inner and outer worlds, and to Marty Burnett, whose evocative photographs on the cover helped us name our book.

Susan Bright and Margo LaGattuta
Editors, Plain View Press

Wind Eyes

Who cares what is behind the curtain?
Write about the bear standing in front looking inside.
The bear loves the snowy fringe of the curtain.
She knows no two curtains are the same.
She knows no two curtains exist.
You cannot find the wind; it will find you.
Ride on its white pillowed back across continents and islands,
oceans and lakes. Trees toss whirligigs in a mad dance.
It all happens before the fall.
Someone lets the bats and bears out, and they fly into the teeth,
gleaning, gleaning bits of your altered blood, savoring your DNA,
swapping tales of victory under the horns of a potent moon,
remembering all of us by moonlight, testing each within this laced
and open wind eye.
I am wind. Open your lids and let me in.
I blow in your eye and tell you stories you do not want
to hear. If you open your window, the whole world will
come in. Trains and swallows and people's hearts will
come in. If you don't know what to do,
serve them marmalade and Earl Grey tea.
Like a breeze, a poem does not know you want it,
will turn corners, come when you call by opening a window.
Wind eyes burn, our eyes burn
when we stand in the white sands at high noon.
The admission of air is dangerous: Breezes do a quick step
through the museum. They are booted children
poking robots when they're scheduled for the dinosaurs.
Air is blazé, sardonic, devil-may-care —
the first goat across the bridge —
followed by Light and Trouble—
unafraid of unabridged trolls.
The point is to think like an eight-headed saint,
look out of the eyes of radically different souls,
let the wind blow across spirit, spin us whole.

Photo by Daryl Bright Andrews

Photo by Bruce Michael Miller

Photo by Daryl Bright Andrews

To the eyes in the heart of the soul

Photo by Bruce Michael Miller

Photo by Bruce Michael Miller

Photo by Daryl Bright Andrews

Right to left: Bruce Michael Miller (photographer, father of Forest, husband of Patricia Albrecht), Daryl Bright Andrews (son of John C. Andrews and Susan Bright, Plain View Press teenager), John C. Andrews (co-publisher and co-owner of Plain View Press, chef), Skye Hibbard, Forest William Meade Albrecht Wallenstein Miller.

I Couldn't Leave Them

Ann Louise Williamson

The pairs of quanta
blink open and shut,
like lions and tigers,
like giant yellow eyes
out there in the dark . . .

I want to put different ideas and images next to each other. This is how I write. If I go too far out, I will see where I might go with the next poem, or the next draft . . . sometimes I put things away for months.

I often look for images in science. This has helped me increase my vocabulary of images and words. Give yourself this exercise: look up the words, quanta and quantum. The words are in general use today, and they have the added glamour of a Greek heritage. Borrow your kid's science book for an evening. I suggest you jot down a few facts and change something—size, color, time span. Translate the facts into a proverb, or a rule for sports, or try a religious way of looking at the facts. What kind of a painting would you make of the facts you jotted? Find a poem or an article about the quantum to see how another writer has worked with the subject. . . in the poem above, I changed the size first, which led to the picture of the giant eyes of wild cats. This led to exposing an old fear of mine from childhood.

Photos by Daryl Bright Andrews

Milk

A woman walks down the hall at two in the morning,
she has to feed the baby, and the baby is crying.
She loves the baby and the baby is crying.
The woman walks into the room, she picks up the baby,
holding him close to her body, and then in her arms,
a little away, she rocks him. Softly, she speaks to the baby,
and brings him back to her body, walks to the bathroom
to get water for washing; she walks to the change table
and unsnaps the sleeper, leaving his arms in the terry sleeves.
She uncovers his legs and feet. Those feet!
Those feet make it all worth it. The baby's hands are greedy,
can already grasp her finger, but his feet are bashful,
like pocket pets from the dime store in her hands.
The woman lets them free and changes the baby,
singing the piggy poem to his toes. She sings it so often,
the baby believes his toes travel while he sleeps,
go to market for roast beef and come crying, *wee, wee, wee,*
all the way home. The woman believes it herself,
but her mind is wobbly from mother's milk.

Little Birds

We are babies. We are lying on our backs,
pulling our toes, as we do every morning,
when someone puts our hands together,
pat-a-cake, pat-a-cake!

Our hands are little birds,
paired for life. They love each other,
they chase and play catch
in the sky in front of our eyes.

Time goes by. We are sitting at tables
stirring up colors when someone takes our hands.
One hand may paint with the brush,
the other must be content to hold the cup.

The birds fly out of our hands,
one to perch on the left cerebral hemisphere,
the other to perch on the right.
Separated for life, they never seek other mates.

Ann Louise Williamson

The Flowers the Sky

For the mother, always at home, nothing was boring,
there was the boy, the house, the perennials someone
before her had planted inside the fence; there was a day
she wasn't looking, but the repairman was looking
and came right away to say to her,
Look who is watering the flowers inside the fence,
and she saw the tee shirt and pants, the new shorts,
the sandals with buckles . . . all of them . . . scattered
across the grass, and she saw her son watering
the perennials. Could they keep on blooming,
would the dog stop nosing the underside and top
of every petal, and would her son water them again . . .
his small clothes in an embarrassing confusion
all over the grass. And the repairman coming to say,
Look out the window, that is how a wild wolf
marks it's territory! A wolf in the wild
mapping out the place it occupies, and a little boy also,
in summer, watering flowers inside the fence
as much as he gets the chance. But the next summer,
he does not water, he watches the sky,
running outside to wave at his father, who rides
in an airplane all week in the sky.
The sky, a place the boy might be invited to,
if anyone understood how lonely he is
watching the back of a father's coat disappear,
and the metal steps fold into the plane's belly,
watching the propellers nose the plane
down the runway until it surprises everyone
and takes off into thin air.

Ann Louise Williamson

Relinquishing Snow

There is a last snow, a thin cover,
when I look at the trees across the swamp
to see how the land lies, how the deer vanish
into the valley only to flash into sight
on the small hill behind the edge of the wood.
Soon April and then her sister May, move in,
their decor all fuzzy wallpaper and green shag
with little flowers set out like knickknacks;
and, of course, May invites me in for tea
and ends up hiring me as her domestic;
she needs help to tidy up for summer people
and someone to lead tours to the beach,
to the antique barns and quaint boutiques.
May, and then her daughter, June, I couldn't
leave them, and where to go? I run back to the porch
swatting at mosquitoes; someone has to stay and daub
the midnight poison ivy rash, and detach the tick
tight in the child's scalp: someone has to get up
before the birds every morning, there are so many
little tender ones that need protection from the cat.

Ann Louise Williamson

Baby Birds

A child comes into the living room
on the first morning of the new year
to see what the grownups have left her.
On a white plate shaped like a leaf,
are chocolate covered caramels
she doesn't like to eat, but how delicious
to feel the little waves patterned
on top of each piece she licks
and puts back, and she finds mixed nuts
which she sorts back into kinds,
melting nuts, one at a time, on her tongue,
until the salt is gone and she can bite
into the plain taste of the nutmeat.
In the kitchen, upside-down
on toweling, balance champagne glasses,
three of them, unused by the guests.
She takes one slowly, carefully,
because these glasses are numbered
in a set of twelve and to break one
would be as naughty as to break them all,
like the first of twelve princesses
carried off to a distant kingdom
by a heartless bridegroom.

The child gets water at the sink
and opens the bucket of ice
she had filled for the party . . .
the fat ice wedges have melted
into transparent slices so fragile
they break at the lightest touch
of her fingers. It would be useless
to put them back in the freezer. . .
like baby birds fallen out of the nest,
their mothers don't want them back.
How can mothers be like that?
Like children ushered off planes
by flight attendants, coming home
after Christmas vacation; they know
their hair is fixed all wrong,
a mother won't like it,
and in clothes a father made them wear,
his new wife bought the whole outfit.

Ann Louise Williamson

The End of August

By the end of August, everything Grandma owned
ended up on the screened-in porch where she lived
all summer behind a green wall of juniper trees.
It was cold eating supper out there, so she gave
my sister and me jackets left over from when
our father was her child. We had to warm up
the sleeves from hanging so long in the closet.
We made our own sandwiches out of anything we
wanted from the refrigerator, and Grandma moved magazines
and flower pots to make room for our dinner plates.
She asked us questions, and we had to answer over the
black and white TV. When it was time for Grandma's
real programs, my sister and I got pillows and scatter rugs
and played with toys from the basement.
We were too old for it, but we made monster cars and freaks
out of snap-together blocks; we cannibalized the ones
that broke and made new monsters, curling up our legs
in shorts, trying to get them inside our father's jackets.
Summer was over when Dad came to get his mother's
furnace running. My sister and I helped carry everything
inside the house . . . lamps and chairs and the old TV crowded
in the kitchen until Grandma knew where she wanted them.
The plants, still flowering red and pink, were set out
at the curb to wait for the rubbish.
My sister and I camped the last night in the living room
watching color TV. We made cinnamon toast and finished up
the pop Grandma said she could never use all by herself.
The cat stayed home for the first time all summer, sitting
by the kitchen wall, staring and listening. Mice were
coming into the heated house from the cold, field mice
piling up behind the plaster like potato chips.

Green

Oh, this is a spring of ominous green,
the green is awake too early
and grumbling through the undergrowth
at the edge of a deep wood.
Long, sticky, green tongues catch the tops of tulips,
reds and pinks disappear overnight.

This green is like the dangerous dreams
that come to fifth grade boys,
the ones who check out books about Tyrannosaurus Rex
week after week from the library.

I fear this green grows weary and vulnerable to wicked advice,
like an underpaid servant girl
listening to her boyfriend's whispers
about a drop of green poison in my soup every night.
I grow dizzy and confused . . .
green spots in front of my eyes.

But this green will not end even there.
The foolish girl doesn't realize she's pregnant,
soon she'll be able to stomach nothing but green
lettuce that grows in my garden,
then she will let down her long hair every evening
like the sun letting down long yellow braids of light
through all this murky green.

Oh, round girl with a head as blank as the sun
and a belly as heavy as the moon,
who do you think will climb up to you,
will it be the witch or the cold-blooded boy?

A la mode

Devil's food
on a gold

rimmed plate.
A la mode.

Eve would
find an

idle man,
Give back

the apple
and bite

into this.
A woman

bides her
time. Adam's

descent by
chocolate.

As She Tosses and Turns

This pain is something new to her,
not a pain in her body,
but an ache that seems located *in* the mattress . . .
right in the middle of the mattress.
As she tosses and turns,
the part of her body resting on that spot hurts . . .
first the side of her chest,
and when she turns over, her back,
and finally a stomachache
as she curls around the place of pain.
She begins to understand
how people come to believe in dangerous rays,
rays from aliens, sent without harmful intent perhaps,
focused on earth only to satisfy alien curiosity,
but harmful, nevertheless.
She wishes the aliens would sweep their beam instead,
sweep, from their hovering saucer,
a beam across the night sky
like a search light announcing an automobile dealership.
(How she and her brother used to sweet talk their dad
to get him to drive to that light,
to drive to that place of car salesmen
who tied balloons with strings around the wrists of children.)
Oh, this is the longest night.
The pain does not leave her, and
she waits for morning and the sun,
that big, irresistible ball of helium
the aliens will want for their kids.
They will pull up their beam
and fly their saucer into that light.

What Will Become of Us All

A woman who has been cleaning apartments all morning
pushes a toy sand bucket filled with kittens across
the animal shelter's counter. She found them this morning . . .
the mother cat must have been taken by the tenants,
but the kittens look healthy, so she's bringing them to the
shelter. She can't keep them; she already has a dog,
(and the newspaper), in her home in the suburbs,
where she feeds the dog and changes his water
and brings the newspaper in for the night, turning the pages
and separating out the shiny advertisements
from the newsprint she saves for the recycle bin.
The dog sits and watches, next to his water dish,
he sits, watching and wondering, *What will become of us all?*
How he longs to ask her about their old age and retirement,
but she doesn't retire; she is a landlady, she drops dead
the next Thursday shampooing carpets, and her sister-in-law
cancels the paper and adopts the dog.
He gets real ice floating in his new water dish
and a toy that looks like meat, and squeaks.
He goes back to the old place anyway and waits for the paper.
The new people never heard of him. They don't let him in.

Ann Louise Williamson

Death

"I think of you as a great king" To Death, Robinson Jeffers

Death, I think of your valley of death
and my father driving his last sedan,
unannounced, across the border.
He stole the car keys to drive there, Death.

I know the look in his eye . . .
the guards would wave him on . . .
why stop trouble at the gate
of the remedy for the world's

troubled? I was the temptation, Death.
I was the rabbit trembling in the gravel
as the wheels spun out of the drive.
I will have my little revenge

when I come. It is evil, I know,
but it is small. In your grave reign
over the valley, Death,
do not fear such a small evil.

February 2, 1996

An Opera With Dog

Ann Louise Williamson

> *Suppose it is a recognized opera.*
> Gertrude Stein

Suppose *this* is a recognized opera, or it could be something wrong at a synapse that fluoxetine could fix. It is unthinkable, but the theatrics are more interesting than if she had a real fire and the house burned down. It has heart, the way a photo of one devout Hopi prying the sun out of the night with prayer and a scattering of seed corn is what you love best in the magazine. The sun comes up on an American woman driving to work, she always turns east at the corner by the bank, and the sun gets in her eyes . . . a blinding light, blackening to red, and red again, fringed now in yellow, then, a velvet calm, in which she sees her dog as clearly as if she hadn't left the house. The dog is sleeping at the bottom of the steps; he lifts his head . . . the woman curses, shakes her own head to get her mind back on the road. Traffic is terrible, and her mind is running away home where the shaggy head turns, snout pointing, nose pumping air. The dog stands, back legs shaking like bad weather, scratches at the door and whines, tail between his nervous legs. He paws the door's glass. Red fire crackles, smoke swallows what she can see of the dog; the dog howls in pain. The woman shivers, opens the car window . . . the dog barks . . . this is the part where the woman gives up, turns the car around, drives home to see if this is the morning she forgot to unplug her curling iron.

She drives, life passes in front of her eyes . . . the coffee, the long
skirt she picked out because of those weird chairs at today's meeting,
eye shadow, blush, plug the curling iron in, sweater over the head,
curling her hair, finished, and then, then . . . she can't remember
pulling the plug, the iron might be next to a Kleenex, the paper
burns, falls to the rug, that fancy doorstop with the dried flowers
goes up like tinder . . . why doesn't she ever worry about this until
she turns east? Is it her Karma or some bargain her unconscious
made with the Angel of Death for whisking that nasty breast crumb
out of her last mammogram? Oh she doesn't have time to worry
about that now . . . she drives, she hears the dog. Fire is eating her
dog alive! She pulls into the drive, leaves the engine running . . .
the dog doesn't move out of her way anymore. It's the same every
morning, like snooze radio that never really wakes you up, she runs
right past him up the steps, she runs down the steps right past him.
She's late for work. He knows a little psychology, but it's hard for a
dog to think up a childhood that could bring this on. Or, suppose it
is a recognized opera, he doesn't speak Italian or German. He sighs,
he rolls over. She forgot to say, *Good dog*, and give him a biscuit.

Ann Louise Williamson

Estrogen Replacement Therapy

We are old women, dead
women to be sure, dead
at seventy, eighty, dead
many years after menopause,

but we are a generation
of women replenished by estrogen,
estrogen cleverly extracted
from the urine of mares, estrogen
rinsing our blood lipid profiles
and percolating calcium into our bones,
estrogen nourishing our post climacteric mucosae.
Yes, we are old women, dead

women beseeching the gates of paradise,
but unchanged from the women we were
when our children left for university
and our husbands joined country clubs

just to have places to show us off dancing.
How our mothers in heaven stir
and fret to see us. Angelic and incontinent,
they hold out their old angel arms,

bones snowing like Christmas.
They want to see us up close,
and oh we *are* rosy and no hairs on our chins
or upper lips shiny from waxing!

The Christ Hospital, 1961

A student nurse was assigned to sit with you and record your pulse and respirations every quarter hour, your blood pressure every thirty minutes. The door to your room was closed; the head nurse insisted upon this. The window shades were down, and the light over the chair left shining. There were no machines then, with their brutal, ineducable heartbeats, only the student pumping the sphygmomanometer's cuff around your arm and the sigh as she released the pressure. There was the sound of the girl's uniform, which did not rustle like ordinary cloth, but was bending, bending in its starch like the stiff white paper that was packaged inside of new shirts. One of the pleasures of your life had been the morning of a new shirt, the department store bag waiting on your highboy. You gave yourself a little more time to dress because of finding all the straight pins, carefully sticking each one into the pincushion next to your wife's hairbrush. Soundless, a pin drops to the floor! You try to turn your head, try to adjust your eyes and catch the glint of metal, to see the sharp pin and pick it up for love of the tender, bare feet of your wife, of your child, of your pet. You unbutton the shirt, removing the stiff white paper that bends in your hands with a flat sound. Startled, you notice the shirt is not in your hands. You feel the student's fingers catch your wrist and the cuff constrict your arm and slowly let go. Will all this careful monitoring keep you alive one moment more? Suddenly you want to live, even if only one moment longer! Your eyelids flutter, but the student doesn't see you, she understands nothing of your life, she is young and knows very little about her own life, and she is so young, and may you forgive her.

November

Ten o'clock in the next morning and still raining, the colors on the wet leaves are like splashing water on my face, bringing up cheek color, putting off rouge until afternoon errands, but the sky is steel and there are frost warnings on the radio. Already my old age has moved into the apartment next door. She comes pleading almost every day to look in my coat closet, where she hears her daughter through her side of the wall, *Help, Mama, I can't get out, I'm hungry, Mama.* I show her my closet has no lock, I shove the coats down the rack, she can look for herself. Usually she lets me throw out the food she kept over night from her supper. I wash the plate, I try to distract her . . . sometimes pictures of my own kids satisfy her, sometimes I make tea and we look at the knickknacks I keep for when I have grandchildren . . . the rain stick from New Mexico, the carved turtle that moves its head, the stones from the beach I keep in a glass of water to show off their colors . . . sometimes she remembers herself and gets terribly embarrassed. Sometimes nothing helps.

And it scares me, what could cause an old lady such worry? Did she punish her girl by locking her in a closet, and then read a child psychology magazine that said it was worse than hitting? Did she get after her for not losing baby fat in time for a big sister's wedding? It could start out innocently enough, like the way I always say my son is in the CIA, from that time his father and I made him sit at the dinner table until he ate all his peas or limas or whatever. That little boy did not cry, did not even fidget. His father and I gave up and sent him to bed, and now I tease him that he could be tortured and never tell the secrets, and why is he always getting transferred or sent to New York? The last time he came home, there were men working on the phone lines across the street and a small engine airplane circled the house. I told him that I know it's The Company. *God, Mom, you'll be saying that in the old folks home and scaring the nurses!* And I will, I will. I'll think the smoke detector's bugged and the dessert's poisoned. A spooky old mind, but preserved, like those leaves kids iron under wax paper after science club nature hikes.

An Egg

"You, little white egg"
Frank Hammerschmidt

An egg is such an old sky of bad weather,
one dull yellow sun and never a rainbow,
but an egg holds the promise of wings,
wings that will feather and fly to good tidings.

Good news, the last coin, the coin in the pocket
of the old man who could be anyone's dad,
the coin he keeps against the day
when the worst that could happen, happens,
that coin, rolled up in a sock, remains.

Rolled up in a sock, the gold wedding band
is left, stuffed into the bosom
of the woman homesteading in a public lobby.
The night watchman makes his rounds,
gives her a can of pop, escorts her to the door.
She squawks like a chicken pushed out of the nest,
a dove pushed out by the ark's keeper.

The keeper of the night continues his watch,
when the sun comes up, his watch is over.
He clocks out, walks home, turns on the TV news.
He cracks an egg into a glass of beer,
drinks his breakfast. He feels better, now he can sleep.

Ann Louise Williamson

What the Universe Looks Like From Earth

What the universe looks like from earth
is a child sitting in her mother's kitchen
inside the Milky Way,
and spreading all around her,
inside out, the universe is flying away.
The taillights are cozy red,
and the earliest galaxies crowd up
in the farthest place to see,
and the earliest, earliest, the Big Bang,
is like a giant rim where everything starts.
The whole wide sky is just a little bit warm,
even the people in China standing on their heads
on the other side of the world
are noticing that the wide sky of the universe
is not completely cold,
and the child's mother is slicing
thin red fish out of a single tomato,
fish as beautiful as the rare carp
beloved of the empress of China,
and the child is swallowing each one alive.

Rose Dust

Patricia Alice Albrecht

"It's what you don't say, that'll kill you," editor Jack Grapes paraphrased from the bible, and I've adopted it as my current mantra. My attempts at writing are always to help me clarify my emotions and heal. If by reading my work you may also feel healed, perhaps I will fulfill my purpose.

Photo by Bruce Michael Miller

Thank you, Bruce, for badgering me to expand, for sharing my vision, and encouraging me to write. Thank you, Forest, for sharing your second birthday with that of my first anthology and confining your artistic expression to paper when rooms of white wall space tempted your muse.

I acknowledge and thank the group of writers at The Writer's Bloc West in Los Angeles, where I adopted a jump-start for writing called "Six Lines." Each week we'd pick a word with the understanding that anyone can write at least six lines based on one word. Rose Dust was triggered by the word "rose." "Six Lines" has spawned numerous scenes for actors, short stories, books and screenplays. Almost all of my titles still contain the word that prompted the piece. Like Ruidoso, the "Noisy River," stories travel far from their source and the adventure is compelling.

Photo by Daryl Bright Andrews

Rose Dust

Eight-year-old Faye Ann sat with her bare legs dodging the ripped edges of the split, Naugahyde back seat of her Dad's brown and white '56 Chevy.

"Turn here." Her Mom pointed for her father to pull into the tree-shaded, gravel parking lot alongside a white, wooden building that resembled a church. In the distance Faye Ann watched the sun make diamonds on Lake St. Clair.

"Arlan, button your jacket." Her dad instructed her little brother, while squeezing into his own seersucker, and leading them up the steps.

Inside, the somber place smelled of roses. Faye Ann had never in her life seen so many yellow, white and red bouquets with banners stretched across them that read, "*Loving Aunt,*" "*Dear Cousin*" and "*Beloved Wife.*"

"Oh, there's Uncle Joe." Her mother, launched through a sea of cousins, towing her dad behind.

"Are you gonna touch her?" Arlan made a face.

"Hush . . ."

"Dare ya."

"You're gross."

"Last one there's a rotten egg." He whispered and disappeared through the crowd towards the casket.

"Arlan!" A fat-cheeked aunt caught him by the shoulder and kissed him profusely, allowing Faye Ann to wind up at the casket first, and oddly alone.

Aunt Marie was lying there, her short dark and semi-graying hair perfectly permed. She had on makeup and red lipstick that matched the roses spilling over the sides of her casket. Black rosary beads were draped around her hands, and it looked like she had dirt under her nails.

Faye Ann sensed a tall dark presence standing behind her. He placed a shaking hand on her tiny shoulder. Faye Ann didn't jump. She knew it was Uncle Joe. He was wiping his eyes under his glasses.

"What's she got her glasses on for?"

"Oh, so she can get around in heaven."

"Oh." Faye Ann nodded, still inspecting.

"She's wearing the dress she married me in."

"She's got dirt under her nails, Uncle Joe."

He peered at her. "Well, by golla." And he started to laugh just a bit.

"We was gardenin' yesterday mornin'. You know how she loved the trellis. And I told her, now, Marie, watch you don't upset the bees. And she says Joe, *'It's my roses, I'll fight 'em to the death if I have to for my perennials.'* And there she was swattin' at the damn things with a measly fly swatter, cussin' the daylights outta God's needed creatures and straddlin' the ladder and the trellis like a spider. And I started laughin' at the sight of her fanny jigglin' like a Jello mold every time she'd swat at a pesky bee. And she says, *'Now, don't get me to laughin', too, I got the gas somethin' fierce, I'm liable to explode us all to kingdom come.'* And I says, better use it on the bees, save me the expense of gettin' an exterminator. Naw . . . Faye Ann, that's not dirt under her nails, that's just rose dust."

Instinctively Uncle Joe reached for Faye Ann's hand and together they covered Aunt Marie's, patting her gently.

"That's just rose dust."

Hoola Popper

It was a muggy August evening at the cabin, and Dad was down by the lake.

"Can I help you bail the boat?" I asked.

"Naw, its almost done."

"I'll get your tackle box," I offered energetically.

"Naw, let your brother, I don't want you to trip coming down the hill."

I shooed myself away to the rope swing and pretended I was an aerialist being watched by an adoring crowd; and sitting on the sidelines would be someone special who loved me. Today I'd pick dashing Randy Rogan, a twelve-year-old, sensitive man of steel.

Earlier that day, I made the mistake of trying to crawl into the hammock with my dad.

"Now, you're a little too big for that, don't you think?"

I didn't think so. I was smaller than my brother, Eddie, by twenty pounds; and he was nine, two years younger than I.

From a distance I could hear the hum of a car driving through the woods. I ran to the outhouse.

My parents used to call Dan Rogan the "Indian," because he was so tall, and red-tanned. He was my dad's buddy, and his wife, Doris, was *"no bigger than a minute."* She and my Mom would get together and laugh just like the dads would. Their kids were similar in ages to us. None of them interested me, except Randy. He was two months older than me, and usually hung around with Eddie. They came to fish. I hid behind the big birch by the outhouse and watched them talk.

Randy got out of the cab of their truck and limped around the back to pull out his mounds of fishing gear.

"What happened?" Eddie asked.

"Cut my big toe off while I was cutting the grass," he answered with a rather heroic, but sad, look on his sweet face.

"No kidding?"

"Yeah, the grass was a little slippery when I went to start the motor, and my foot slipped underneath." He looked around to see how close the dads were before whispering, "It hurt like hell."

"Eeeyew." Eddie paled.

"Yeah, I got twenty-three stitches, wanna see?"

Eddie just shook his head no. "I just ate."

"Yeah, its kinda gross looking. Still hurts a little. Sometimes I feel this itch though, and there's nothing there to scratch."

"Eeeyew." Eddie made a sickly face.

My heart melted in sympathy, and I floated towards them feeling like this angelic nurse was sprouting inside of me. My mission: to do whatever I could to make Randy Rogan feel better after suffering such an horrific loss.

"Hi, Randy." He had deep blue eyes and thick curly brown hair.

"Oh, hi."

"How are you?" I looked down to his foot.

"Alright."

"Yeah?" I swooned over to Dad with a pouting look, and I appealed, "Dad, can I please come fishing with you tonight?"

"Ei, yi, yi! What's the world coming to?"

"I'll sit up front and not get in the way, I promise. Please? Hi, Mr. Rogan."

I figured Mr. Rogan had a soft spot for short women with puny blonde hair because he married one. He looked down at me and smiled.

"Aw, hell, Ed, let her come."

I beamed. I grabbed the cutest looking orange life preserver and was the first one in the boat. I would be useful. I would hoist the anchor. I would even bait Randy's hook if he needed help.

Dad helmed the motor. On the seat in front of him, sat the boys and, in front of them, Mr. Rogan. I sat in the tip of the bow.

Once across the lake, where it was darker and cooler, the mosquitoes started coming out. The men greased up with OFF, and I watched Randy spray it on his hands and rub it on his face like after-shave. The mosquitoes loved Eddie, probably because of all the mayonnaise he put on his bologna sandwiches. He'd wait until they were just settling down to poke their stingers into him; and then "WHAP!" he'd smack them. Sometimes, just to be dramatic, he'd let them take his blood, and then he'd smack them; and his blood would smish all over.

Dad was going to teach the guys how to cast for bass towards the shore. I plopped the anchor down along the edge of the drop-off, and Mr. Rogan rigged a night crawler harness for bluegills. He hung his line over the deep-water side.

"Look at this baby!" Randy took a brand new fire engine red-and-white hoola popper from his tackle box. The five, three-pronged, steel hooks sparkled in the dimming light.

"Better get your scent off it," Eddie instructed and handed him the worm carton. "Dip it in here and get the smell of the worms on it."

"Yeah?"

Dad lit up a cigarette. He opened a beer and tossed one to Dan. We all laughed as it sprayed all over him when he opened it.

Dad began his instruction.

"Ya wanna release the button just at the right moment. O.K.? Like this." And with a flick of his left wrist, Dad made a perfect cast, landing within six inches of the craggy shoreline.

Eddie was already a junior expert and aimed his lure towards the north end, it's high arch breaking through the sky like a comet before cracking the smoothness of the lake's quiet surface.

The quiet was only interrupted by the whirl of reels winding in rhythm: *tug, tug, reeeel . . . tug, tug, reeeel*.

Randy was ready to begin his cast. His first cast ended up in a loud thud as it crashed into the outside of the boat, missing Dad's knee by five inches.

"It's a new reel for me."

"We can see that." Dad smirked.

I smiled encouragingly at him. He tried not to look embarrassed. His second cast went straight up and up and up and landed in the branches of an overhanging birch tree. Dad gave Mr. Rogan the "side eye" glance as he tried to contain his laughter. Mr. Rogan just kept looking across the lake towards the cabin. In the distance, we could hear polkas on Mom's radio.

Randy tugged and tugged and yanked, his rod straining to the point of breakage. All of us winced in anticipation, not knowing where his hoola popper would land when it came shooting back out of the trees at us.

"Maybe we better just cut the line," Dad suggested.

"Aw, no, it's my best lure."

"We'll get ya another one."

"Jeez."

Dad cut his line and we watched the birch snap back to attention.

"Looks like it's wearing an earring," I quipped, batting my eyelashes, but he didn't see me.

"Yeah, it does," Eddie laughed.

"Here, try this one." And Dad pulled out an emerald, metallic special that was one of his prize possessions. The ashes on his cigarette got long, as it dangled from the corner of his mouth while he tied the popper onto Randy's line.

"Dunk it in the worms," Eddie said.

Randy did and we tried not to watch him cast. He swung the rod behind him and practiced flicking his wrist.

I said a silent prayer to Saint Peter, who, I hoped, was the patron saint of fishermen.

Dad lifted his gold, golf cap, smoothed back his curly brown hair and put it back on and immediately screamed. "Ow, ow, ow!!!"

We all looked at Dad, except Randy, who was trying to get his reel to fly. Randy kept yanking, but Dad was grabbing at the back of his head. He came off his seat like somebody was lifting him by the scruff of the neck, yelling, "Ya got me! Ya got me!"

"Holy mackerel!" Mr. Rogan handed me his rod to reel in, grabbed a knife and cut the line.

Randy was white. Eddie was silent. Mr. Rogan was stunned, and I was getting a tugging on Mr. Rogan's line.

"Oh, nooo," I wanted to cry.

"It's o.k., o.k," Dad reassured me. He shook his head.

"Turn around," Mr. Rogan asked Dad.

"Man!"

"Guess I got a hoola poppa hangin' from my obdula oblongata," Dad laughed, to help us all feel like he wasn't going to die on the spot.

I gasped at the sight. I wanted to faint, but the rod started bending. "I think I got one."

"Reel it in!"

"It's too big."

"It's yours, come on."

"Oh, please," I cranked halfheartedly. My dad was wounded and was watching me.

"Come on, you know how, show the boys."

And I kicked into action. I got mad. I followed that flailing fish around the boat and back again, kept it away from the motor, and I played the little sucker until it tired out.

"All right! All right, atta girl! Bring her in, bring her here," Dad was coaching me.

I reeled in a beautiful blue gill the size of Mr. Rogan's face and brought her into the boat without a net. Dad took the hook out and set her in the bottom.

"Way to go," Eddie cheered.

"I've never seen one that big." Randy was shocked.

"Bring up the anchor." Dad said. "We better get back."

Nervously I struggled, but the anchor was knotted in weeds.

"Why don't you sit back here with me," Dad said.

Mr. Rogan pulled up the anchor with two fingers while Dad pull-started the engine, aimed the boat home, and put his arm around me, his hoola popper dangling from the back of his head twinkling in the twilight.

Skipping

I saw the shape
of a shy boy
skipping down the street,
the weight of school books
piled high on his expanding shoulders.

I smiled at him
noting his delight . . .

But he stopped.

His face drained into condemnation,
personifying the beast
of a newly forming, vacant man.

Patricia Alice Albrecht

Wing Tips

It took three men standing in wing tips:
one black, one brown, one taupe with tassels;
and I thought of you, Dad.
I suddenly saw you as one man—
one against the mass of millions.
I saw you small and trying.
For the first time I sensed you as a man—
not my dad,
not the drunken ogre,
not the one who unknowingly hurt.
But a man who tried and tried and lost.

I remember the time you got your last pair of wing tips
smooth luggage loafers.
How you walked around in them, on the oval braided rug,
over the hardwood floors, out to the grass.
Smiling, happy, proud . . .
a man with dreams, whose wings
would not carry.

Patricia Alice Albrecht

Just a Second Before . . .

Just a second before . . .
we were chatting about nothing,
and I tried to make you laugh
to forget your puppy's death.

And in all that time before . . .
the sun began to bake a new June day,
and the squirrels teased the spaniels
and little Al, laughing,
spun in the shade on the tire swing;
we battled bees.
Sisters, laughing,
we sanded Mother's house.

In all that time before . . .
so much life was living
so simply and uncomplicated
and free and guiltless
and goddamned normal!

Then we began the end of you,
and the awfulness
hammered me with
ball pein, blunt dumb, numbness.
When you fell on me
keening *"eeeeeeeeeeeeeeee."*
I laughed at you for your fear of bees,
until I touched your leg
   and felt the silent, searing buzz
of electricity
ripple through you.

I
am
so tired
I
could die
but
first
I have
to do
the dishes.

Happy Happy Birthday Baby

All day Claudia walks lost in the fog of her dream. An unknown woman being hit by a car replays in her mind.

At four forty-five p.m. the clouds darken. Too far from home and her messy kitchen, she stops in Cafe Figaro, orders stragiatele soup and sits alone, compares her dwindling savings account balance against a growing Christmas list. A wave of nausea follows. "Oh God, if only I were dead," she thinks.

A fiery bolt of lightning cracks through dark clouds. Claudia cowers with the thunder.

From behind her a woman approaches. She wears a black leather jacket and close-cropped hair. "Are you waiting for someone?" the woman asks.

"No." Claudia jumps

"Would you care to join me?"

Caught off guard Claudia says "No, thank you," and drips honey on her bread. L.A. is not the place a stranger asks you to her table unless she has something else in mind, she thinks.

Claudia sips soup, sorry the choices she made in the past thirty-nine years still leave her in such disarray. Raindrops pummel the pavement, driving self-made demands through her head. She has too many incomplete projects, little or no time to visit with friends, much less her boyfriend Marc. She is so tired and attributes it to pre-birthday depression. Every day she comes home determined to finally clean the pile of dirty dishes, bills and research articles, but somehow the soft folds of the couch always win out . . . and the image of herself flopped on the couch only reminds her of her sister, Lorraine.

Lorraine had too many kids too young and always left too many chores undone. Claudia used to clean Lorraine's house. She thought her sister was a slob.

Claudia is turning forty. She denies that turning forty is some big deal. Her sister Lorraine always said, "Now when you turn forty we'll really celebrate. Leave the kids with our husbands and fly off to a tropical island, sun on the beach, drink Mai Tai's and have muscled young natives fan us with feathers . . . when you're forty."

But Claudia, unlike Lorraine, had never had three kids, never gotten married and still lives. So much has happened since Lorraine died. Most of Claudia's contemporaries no longer get sun tans, no longer drink, and, well, the whole idea of getting fanned by strapping young natives is so politically and socially unacceptable . . . so much has happened since Lorraine died.

It pours. Cars dodge airborne debris like earthbound fighter pilots. Claudia finishes her soup as the unknown woman in the black leather jacket winks, walks past her and out the door. She dashes across the street, but not before a car clips her from behind. There is a collective scream from inside the restaurant. The waiter runs out with a towel and Claudia, gasping for breath, feels caught between wanting to run out to help the woman and wanting to close her eyes and wish it had been herself. She closes her eyes and sees, instead, the dream . . . the piece of dream that has haunted her all day . . . this woman being hit by a car.

Claudia looks out the window. The woman moves. Claudia assumes she'll be o.k. Swiftly, she pays her bill and leaves.

Rain coats the windshield like syrup. Claudia feels guilty. *"Maybe I should have said 'yes', who knows who she was . . .what she wanted. Why did she want to sit with me?"*

Claudia struggles for breath, is on the verge of tears as she ascends the steps to her Studio City duplex. Lightning cleaves the sky and the wind tangles her keys. She hears her radio playing.

Once inside, she smells the hauntingly familiar scent of honeysuckle and shakes her head *no*. She smells her sister's cologne, the scent Lorraine always wore, the last scent she associates with her sister before the others that followed, the smells of vomit and burnt flesh.

Claudia drops her bags and still smells the honeysuckle. She locks herself inside her apartment to escape the memories the smell induces. A bolt of lightning brightens the sky, and thunderous echoes follow, then the buzz of a whining transformer sparks out. Everything electrical is dead and all she hears is running water.

"Marc?"

There is no answer.

"Marc?"

She hears dishes clink together on the drain board and cautiously steps around the corner to look inside her kitchen. A candle flickers from within. Another crack of lightning strafes the kitchen, and the shadow of a large round woman blackens the wall. A woman with red hair stands at the sink.

Claudia sinks to the floor with the wind knocked out of her for the second time that evening.

The woman turns slowly around. "Rainey?"

"I can't believe, you of all people, have turned into such a slob!" Lorraine says.

"I'm not . . . I'm not . . . its just that lately . . ." What is she saying? Her sister has been dead for fifteen years, and they are arguing housekeeping. "How did you get here? I mean . . . how are you? How are you . . . oh Rainey . . . " and she crawls over to hug her sister's legs. "I'm so sorry I couldn't save you . . . I didn't know . . . I'm sorry I laughed at you while you were . . ."

"I know . . . I know . . ." Lorraine said. She hugs back but not long enough for Claudia to feel complete.

"Look at you! Look at you!" Claudia sputters. "You look great! But . . . but . . . I'm older than you now. Rainey . . . oh Rainey . . so much has happened. You should see your kids, Rainey. You're going to be a grandmother!"

"I know." Lorraine was always the calm in the face of a storm.

"How did you get here? I have to call Mom."

"No. I don't think she's ready for this just yet." Lorraine scrubs the silverware.

"I can't believe you're here. You always hid from thunder."

"Guess it can't get me now." Lorraine said.

"How? Why?"

"Well, every so often, we get, like, a special dispensation. We get to come back. Not usually to someone we know, but sometimes it happens, you know . . . those unexplained mysteries when someone comes out of plane wreck alive or something."

"Do I get to die now, too?" Claudia asks.

"Ha! No." And Lorraine belts out cacophonous laughter, a sound long missed and nearly forgotten.

Claudia has mixed feelings about her response. "Have you seen your kids, Lorraine? You'd be amazed."

"Well, I did want to know about Dylan."

"He was in an accident."

"Yeah. When he passed out at the wheel, I got to steer the truck onto the island, but since then?"

"You saved him? You were there? That's amazing!"

"I just steered the car; how is he now?" Lorraine wants to know something. Claudia isn't sure how to answer. "He doesn't seem to drink so much. But you must know everything, don't you?" Claudia is certain.

"No . . . only some things, like everybody else, but what I may know for some people in particular may make them think we know everything, but no, I'm not omnipotent yet." Lorraine scours a pot.

"Why did you die like that in front of me?" Claudia asks.

"Sometimes it takes high voltage to get you to see the light."

"What wasn't I seeing?"

"All of you. All of who you are and what you are capable of being and doing."

"So watching you get electrocuted was supposed to wake me up? What about you?"

"I chickened out. My life wasn't working. I chose to leave."

"Well, neither is mine, God, what do I have to do to get out of here?"

"That's why I'm here . . . to tell you it's not about leaving the planet. It's about leaving the little box you packed yourself into."

"My life sucks, Lorraine! I'm almost forty and everything I start gets slapped down. None of my dreams have come true. I don't know what else to do."

"Claudia, believe me . . . that 'nothing good is every wasted' line, is true. I can't help you sort out your life, or promise you a rainbow. They only let me stay long enough to do the dishes."

Instinctively, Claudia pulls a greasy broiler pan from the bottom of the oven. "Here." And she pulls out moldy containers from the refrigerator.

Lorraine faces her sister squarely. "Claudia . . . I'm here to tell you you're pregnant."

"No . . ." Claudia gasps again for oxygen. "I can't be."

"What?"

"I can't . . I'm too, I'm too tired."

"Now you know why my house was always a mess." Lorraine chuckles again.

"But, I'm too incomplete."

"Earth is a work in progress. If it wasn't, no one would ever have to be here."

"No . . your daughter is the one who is pregnant, they must have gotten something mixed up there."

"No . . I know about Angie . . I got to catch her head when she passed out from morning sickness in August. I got to hold her for five minutes before Jimmy found her. I got to hold her."

Distant thunder weights the silence.

"Look, this broiler has to soak, they're not going to let me stay."

Claudia slumps into the kitchen chair and drops her head into her arms on the table.

"I'm telling you Claudia, don't do what I did. Don't give up because you're scared or feel defeated. That's what they want you to do." Lorraine swats a dark corner of the kitchen with a dishtowel, as if fending off a fly.

"Who?" Claudia sits up.

"The darkness . . . " Lorraine unties her apron. "Look, dishes are one thing, but mold isn't part of the deal. Will you give everybody a hug for me at the Christmas party?"

"How will they know?"

"It has to last more than two seconds then they'll know for sure it's not you." Lorraine looks kindly at her younger, now older sister. "Look, you always had the balls in the family. Don't drop this one." she says placing her hand on her sister's stomach. "You're gonna be fine . . . believe in that for a change . . . its o.k. to trust again."

"Rainey . . .what about . . . there was this girl and an accident I saw just before I came home."

"Well, I was trying to get a decent meal while I was down here, but no, as usual, you had to make things difficult, and I had to do the dishes."

"Thanks . . ." Claudia says. She wants to hug her sister for all the years she missed but edits herself once again.

"Yeah . . . yeah . . . yeah . . ." Lorraine blows out the candle. She rinses her hands, dances out of the kitchen and back to the ether as electricity flickers on and the radio plays . . . "Happy Happy Birthday Baby."

Succulent

Child of the desert
Angel Echeveria
who stole you from your home?

Someone who thought that because you were pretty
you were free to be taken?

Your arms reach for heaven
like little lost peach trees;
your wings weep over the sides of the pot,
mourning the drench
dripping green gooey tears onto my tablecloth
displaced and alone.

And what do the gardening manuals know?
As if enough right light, soil and water
would keep you alive and happy.

I know what's been sucked from you and
there's no way I can blow it back.

I Just Thought It Was Menopause

"My period's late." I said.

Norman looked at me with a grin. "Let's go to the grocery store." He said.

"I'm too tired. I gotta eat dinner."

"What do you want?"

"Liver. Liver and onions." I said.

Now that was not the familiar response of a macrobiotic vegetarian but I had evolved enough in my austerities to know a random deviation could be acknowledged without my health falling apart.

I gulped my meat and we walked home via the feminine hygiene section of the super market to pick out an E.P.T. test. Norman was so blatant. The least he could have done was slip it between some kale and kidney beans but it was the only thing we bought. He preened like a lion wanting the world to know that he was getting laid.

At home, I wanted to take a shower and go straight to bed.

"Noooo . . . we'll light sage and say a prayer and drink sparkling cider while the test is cooking." Norman was heavy into ritual for all occasions, one of the things I love about him, except when I'm too tired to participate.

"It's probably just menopause." I said. I was forty-one and since my mom had early menopause, I figured it must be hereditary.

"Go pee on this." he said, after carefully reading the directions from the E.P.T. kit.

I thought back . . . we used condoms . . . and rhythm . . but we weren't careless . . . (Oh, sure . . . explain that to the judge.)

I sat on the throne while my past dripped its way into my present.

Norman cackled outside the door of the bathroom like a hovering hen. "Come on . . . ."

He acted like Santa was coming and carefully carried the stick to my altar. We prayed and set it there, but would not watch it turn color.

"Magic is magic because it can't be seen." He grabbed my hand and pulled me to his lap while we toasted with our "champagne".

"I have a feeling." He said. He was hoarding marbles of imaginings.

"Yeah, so do I, exhaustion. Honey, I gotta go to bed."

I had kitchen work to be done all over the apartment. And I didn't want to do it.

"Just a little while. We'll never share this moment again. Remember, this time right now, here, like this."

That's what made the moment so memorable I guess. Norman prepared it. The house was a wreck, I felt ugly, but we were on the precipice of a message which could alter our lives forever.

I never wanted to have children. I never wanted to live with anyone. I wanted to be a recognized actress working more than I was but none of my plans were manifesting like they said in the spiritual books and I was loosing hope about how my life might feel enriched.

At seventeen, my Dad died. Two years later I was charged with involuntary manslaughter in a fatal car accident, "no lo contendre," and three years after that my older sister, Marcia, was electrocuted to death while we were painting my mom's house. Marcia left three kids, aged three to five whom I watched while my brother-in-law managed to find a housekeeper. Eventually, he found one and married her within a year, but she disliked my mom. The new wife denied us visits with the kids. During all this, was the salt and peppering of a dysfunctional but loving family I knew I had to escape in order to realize my dreams. I made a huge internal decision. Leave Michigan, head for Hollywood and never get close to anyone again.

My acting career was like a jet that spent more time taxiing the runway than being in the air, and I didn't have the inner fuel to compete with the other airlines.

Twenty years and a lot of therapy later, I finally met an artistic visionary I was willing to trust and decided to love. Norman.

"Come on . . . " We crept back into the bedroom, opening the door like the spirits themselves might actually be playing canasta on the bed, and our entrance might startle them. Norman snuck over to the stick. I would not look.

"Come on, this is your life." He said.

He picked it up. "Says yes . . . "

"No . . ." I said.

"Yes."

"Oh fuck!"

"Really."

"It can't be. I'm too old."

"Guess not." He was elated.

I just exhaled expletives in astonishment. And Norman kissed me, hugged me, kissed me. I surrendered to the idiocy of emotion and let myself be swept away by his passion.

"It's a boy." I was unalterably convinced.

From the beginning of our relationship Norman professed to want to have a child with me. I wanted him to want me. I couldn't see how the two things went together, so I was resentful whenever he said that. Well that, and the fact that he wasn't really talking marriage. We didn't even live together. Which was fine. I loved living alone. I loved writing, having time to obsess. I owned my own condo, in L.A.! A huge real estate victory, even though the market was going soft, and with it my ability to get sufficient acting work to keep me medically insured. But I had things.

What I didn't have was a strong sense of my own family which I cried frequently about. I figured it would come eventually.

The day after the test, I got morning sickness, and the day after that I was sure I looked three months pregnant. My mean weight was 93 lbs. The baby stole all my nutrients and flat stomach. How could I not show?

My vanity, my ego, my independence, my dreams all started to slip away from me. And I didn't like it. I grew mean and could only see the disadvantages. I used to baby-sit my nieces and nephews, I knew how hard it was for Marcia. I couldn't stand to be that compressed. I would die artistically.

My pessimism, negative cash flow, and fear of being a horrible parent made me want to abort. This compounded my guilt, since the majority of my friends needed fertility counseling or adoption and would swap places with me in a minute. I prayed to be accepting, but it was so hard. So hard. All I wanted to do was cancel out any perceptions of what might make my life any harder than it already was.

My close girlfriend, Brenda, brought over a gift book graphically showing the developing fetus. When I couldn't look at the pictures she was hurt. I couldn't look at raw chickens either. While finding a mid-wife, a health practitioner said I needed to be desensitized against the realities of birth. They force fed me bloody embryonic developing fetus pictures. Their poking and prodding hurt like hell. I hated being examined. I hated the whole thing.

Now that Norman had the opportunity for a dream of his to come true, the timing was just bad. He wanted to move to pursue his song writing career. I just wanted to move to get away from my projections. Anger as I never knew it, rose in me with a rage that reminded me of my dad when he got drunk. My greatest fear was of turning out to be a parent like him.

Everyone I talked to was so overjoyed for me. For Norman. When I didn't share in their enthusiasm, I felt like there was something fundamentally wrong with me. I'd crawl into the closet or hide in the shower and sob. There was nothing to hold onto.

Norman tried to convince me to do the noble thing. I wanted to trust God. I wanted to believe that sometimes the things I didn't necessarily plan in my life, just might give me what I needed. But it was all a risk.

We scheduled a CVS test at thirteen weeks. It made a lot more sense to find out if we were carrying a Down's child rather than wait until nearly five months of gestation. The day was December 15th. Marcia's birthdate. Had she lived this would have been something we could have shared. I pretended her back to life and carried her in my heart. I bit my tongue to stifle my fear even though I had no sense of where I was going or how I was going to proceed with my life.

Norman reminded the nurses not to tell us the sex of the fetus. He held my hand and watched the monitor during the procedure. When we saw the little life inside me jump, I smiled. Suddenly this was real. This was a real, little being who had a mission despite whatever propaganda I filled my brain with, despite how many french fries I ate, or what I knew or didn't know about our futures. It didn't matter that the test came back screwed up. It didn't matter that Norman and I had no sense of stability according to the outside world. This little spirit was going to be born whether we liked it or not, despite the thoughts in my head.

In January I was reprieved from nausea. The night of the sixteenth Norman and I were fighting.

"Something's wrong." he said feeling edgy. "You should clean that filthy aquarium." he said. Unlike himself, he left to sleep at his place that night, the first time in weeks.

I woke up about 4:00 a.m. complaining to God about my circumstances.

"What am I going to do? How am I going to get through this? How can I work and take care of a baby at the same time? Why now? Why me? Why does any baby want to come through us?" I bitched.

Spent and hopeless, I lit a candle in the hopes my prayers would be heard. Usually I leave the candle in the tub, but this time I left it exposed on my altar.

Earthquakes are first heard. Distant rattling and shaking increased with volume and intensity. It was *Jumanji* in the bedroom. Glassware, books, crashing was heard all through the place. Bricks, windows, large things fell outside. Car alarms went off, screams from other tenants. I buried myself under the covers and pillows to stay as cushioned as possible. And I made a deal with God.

"O.K., o.k., o.k. I was just kidding before. Life is just fine. I'll do the job. I'll take care of this baby. We're fine here. We're safe. But if you wouldn't mind, please just don't let the aquarium go over or let the candle on the altar blow us up...please?"

I cradled my stomach like a kitten. "We're o.k. baby. We're o.k. We're fine. The house might be wrecked but we're fine. Probably just a little 3.5 right under the carport nothing to worry about."

Then, for the first time in my pregnancy I had this amazingly calm maternal feeling. I knew I would not die. I knew again, this baby would not die.

My knight in his dingy-red pickup raced up the steps within an hour. "I was heading for the freeway, but decided to take the top streets instead." Norman's legs shook; we held each other, waded through debris, and crawled back to bed to catch the aftershocks.

Norman helped me clean up the mess. And I thanked God for keeping the bargain. The aquarium was only half empty, and the candle had stopped on the edge of the table. All important things fell on softer things below. Compared to friends, my damage count was far below everyone else's. A house two doors down was knocked completely off its foundation. Gas mains were erupting. Had Norman taken the freeway, he would have been killed. Others did lose their life in the 6.5+ Northridge quake. We felt protected.

The months to follow were a roller coaster of hopes and fears that I'd ridden all my life. Only now there were three of us sharing the ride. Norman was so thoughtful, he asked his pregnant friends to lend me their clothes. They did. He moved in with me to save money and monitor his progeny. He shelved his personal hopes for greater possibilities.

A month before delivery, we were offered a larger space to live in on a mountain top in Malibu. Eight months pregnant, I moved my life to accommodate someone else. How could I carry a baby when I couldn't even open a pickle jar? Every time I tried to put a car seat together I was reduced to a puddle of tears . . . I had no strength, patience or ability.

I planned to deliver naturally, but after thirty-six hours of irregular contractions and not dilating, I had to go to Cedars Sinai. Fourteen hours and an epidural later, they Heimliched me and out popped a big-headed, baby boy.

He was strong, healthy and pretty. When they put him in my arms I said something profound like "I like him."

And I still do. And I still think one day I'll wake up with all the answers, a guide book on how to direct my life and feel forever freed from the sadness and depression that gets in the way of my being able to love.

Well, I guess, I'm writing my own book and it's the sadness that keeps me human. But it's Norman and that boy who find me laughing at times in the day, when in the past, I'd wind up hidden in the closet.

Today I can sling thirty pounds without flinching and assemble a stroller in five seconds flat.

And just like life here I am, still nursing and I'm starting menopause!!! Something else to moan to God about.

Laces

As you untie
the knots of
my understanding
I'm left holding long laces
of thought
but nothing to cling to.
They're dragging the ground,
getting nicked, wet and shredded;
and I haven't the
strength or know-how
to mend them.
So how do I hold
on to the hope and trust,
when my heart and dreams
unravel to dust?
I don't yet know how
to weave a new life
from the threads of laces
that once knotted
my identity so tightly.

Blue Legs

Blue legs, blue midriff, blue lips.
Clots of blood coming to the surface of the skin
like plum polka dots.

O

Hungry for something, I would settle for a nutty
donut.

O

Mom, nervously scattered her attention trying to help
me dress, do the right thing, not be in the way,
desperately trying to find her place — to fit in — to
feel wanted and I don't take time to put her at ease.

O

"What's really going on?" Jack asks, never content
that I can just be tired. I get mad because he seldom
allows me the simplest emotional deviation as if my
moods could only be acceptable if they hold some deep
psychological reason.

O

After nursing, I roll groggily out of bed, put my pink
sweat pants on backwards and raise the window
blinds. The mother finch flies from her nest in the bird
feeder to hideout in the eaves. The fog drifts thick as
snow.

O

I stuff a whole donut in my mouth so no one sees.

Sometimes I find I'm watching myself breast-feed James, like I was outside of us both, hovering above until I'd touch his little indigo flannel leg and want to cry because I know my touch can never protect him from the pain he'll encounter in his life beyond the crib.

But the donut doesn't help. There is still this empty hole - - this thing that I think can be filled up by food.

I still have to put away my wedding dress. I keep it out of its box

all week, strung up high in the closet so James won't get peanut butter fingers on it. I haven't worn it enough. I haven't been a bride
long enough. I am back to being a reluctant mother, and a daughter,
who cannot decipher the silences of her mother. So I assume what is
wrong and determine "myself" the cause. Then for two long minutes
get to lock myself in the bathroom for prayer, until James comes running to find me, and Jack asks a question. Mother's coffee creams
the air.

And now, pictures of the wedding show my mom, this insecure
satellite walking gingerly around her daughter, me, a midlife bride,
and all I'm thinking is "Where's Jack . . . where's James . . . where
are all the parts?" I walk to my future, holding a parasol instead of
my mother's hand or my father's arm.

"I had my own feelings," she tearfully confesses. "I had my own
feelings."

"But you didn't tell me." I plead.

"I missed your dad not being there. I know this wasn't a
conventional wedding, but I didn't know my place . . . what I was
supposed to do."

And I didn't know either. Like sometimes when I'm all alone
with James while he's playing, I'm watching us, lost somewhere, and
wonder "What am I supposed to do?" I don't know what I'm
supposed to do with him. And how can I do it right? I look for the
mother finch but she has flown off.

I feel horrible at times like that. That's why I have such a difficult
time relaxing at all, anytime, anywhere, especially in bed with Jack.
It always comes down to what am I supposed to do? And how can I
do it right? And it's not like I plan it, but when I'm relaxed, it's as if
someone's opened Batman's Cave and out fly all these old "seeings,"
like the time of the accident when my car collided with a
motorcycle and the girl flew off —over the hood onto the pavement
— her head cracking inside the helmet — blonde hair spilling
everywhere. She wore blue jeans and a cropped top. She was fleshy
around the middle, but young, seventeen. And her boyfriend, legs
all broken, crawled over to her. I was so scared I started to pee my
pants and ran across to the gas station to hideout in the bathroom,
praying for it to all go away. But it wouldn't. She died five days later,

and I was charged with involuntary manslaughter. I was two years older than she and some part of me walked into a freezer and stayed there.

Every so often, after I've tried hard to be on the lookout for any possible thing that might go wrong before it does, I start to thaw out, but it's so messy. Like parts of me just bleed on the floor, and I try to pick them up and contain them, but I don't know how. I don't know who I am and what I'm supposed to do with these gelatinous parts of me. So I have to sleep.

And I feel so sad I didn't hold my mother's hand when I walked around the pond to marry Jack last week. I feel badly I couldn't comfort her when she missed my dad and feel like I slaughtered her deepest feelings because I didn't see her pain.

I hate it that I always feel vacant when people try to get in, but I'm mute. It's a fog that overtakes me.

I don't want my sins to visit upon my son, but sometimes, when I look into his clear blue eyes, my breath is gone with the wondering of what the finches know that I don't? What am I supposed to do for him and how? Always . . . what am I supposed to do? Because I don't want to turn anymore feelings, anymore hopes, anymore people, blue.

Notes From My Top Pocket

Naomi Louisa Mountjoy Long

"Hullo!" I'm an Aussie. I should greet you with "Ow are yer, Mate?" I have lived and worked in the U.S.A. for almost 40 years but I remain Australian from the inside out.

I cannot carry out the luggage that I have stored up in my head. Bringing with me the shoes and socks of hope, the underpants and bras of past experience, the safe covering of jeans, shirts and sweaters and, of course, the hair shampoo — to keep my head clean and clear, you know!

I realize now, these are things which hide me, and I strip myself naked — but I do it inside.

I haven't revealed my soul — I'm afraid of it myself. My life has been built up until now on what people will think of me — so that I am afraid to step out — breasts dangling, stomach breaching out — and bad breath.

But no! Put that all behind! Let me step out from the crevices in cliffs—I will tell my story. I will write of secrets that are hidden in the mountains and deserts of my soul.

I will shout poetry from the barren clifftops.

I will cherish, in childhood wisdom, stories of buds on the trees and the flowers, and I will write about being at one with the moon and stars.

Keep a notebook and pen in your pocket. Wherever you go, inside or out, observe. Is anything moving? How does it move? Where does it go? How do things respond? Write it down in notes. Do birds fly in rhythm? Do insects? Keep your thinking handy and, also, your pen and paper.

Photos by Daryl Bright Andrews

Naomi Louisa Mountjoy Long

I am a Feather

on the wing of a bird.
I hear the flute call my mate.
I am sound waving down the hill,
waving to a higher sound.
Let me swing up, up.
The pine trees reach up.
The flute swings my self into the trees . . .
the pine trees that reach up again.

The breath is nervous,
flutters like the bird's wings.
It reaches for its mother's bounty.
Food for the soul? No!
Food for the body.
The flute carries the soul's food,
carries my imaginings,
floats them up and up.
The sound — the breath
flutters and dies.
I lie quiet, silent.
I can hear the outward breeze.
Is it possible to hear my soul?

Naomi Louisa Mountjoy Long

So! What Nationality Are You?

I flew to the USA almost fifty years ago. Seems
a long time, now, but I can remember it very clearly.

All of us who are Australian on the plane
have to be cleared through customs at the airport
in Hawaii. Inside the building some official lines us up
and gives us an auspicious-looking form to fill out.

Everything is fine until the second-to-last-question—
What race are you?

_____Oriental?
_____Caucasian?
_____Negro?
_____Other?

Now, I have only known myself as Australian,
have never been questioned as to heritage before this,
and Australian is not on the form.
I ask another Australian what he is going to answer,
and he doesn't know. So we are in a quandary.
I know that I am not Oriental; I know that I am not Negro.
I have absolutely no idea what Caucasian is.
Does it have something to do with the Caucasus Mountains
in Europe? And if I say *other*, will *Australian* be enough,
or do they want me to go into a Celtic or Aboriginal background?

So I finally ask.
Oh, you're a Caucasian! the official says.
Thanks, I reply. I still have absolutely no idea
of the link-up between Caucasian, white,
European, or Australian.

In fact, I wonder why we bother with all this.
Aren't we all human?

The Untricking

My brother chases me through the house.
I trick him by locking the door
between our rooms.
I know I put the key
in my handkerchief sachet.
Yet, when I go to untrick
the whole incident—
it isn't there.

Years later, camping with friends
on a stretch of vast coastline,
my mind is on my love.
I hide the car key
in my top pocket.
And we walk—
I'm consumed by the ocean's breadth.
We need the car key, they say.
The key is not there!

Now, in these gray years, walking to the edge
of a tangled life, a voice once again repeats,
And where's the key?

Metamorphosis

We betray ourselves with repetition.
So soon in life
our souls are set.

We live and re-live—
crawl out of a chrysalis
changed, we think,
experience a metamorphosis
of life
for a while.

Repeat. Repeat.
How many times?
Is it always the same?

The significant flowers
remain significant flowers,
and life is repeated.
And life is repeated.
And life is . . . .

Mother's Day

It's the early 1930's, and Australia is a bit slow at picking up and copying the celebrations of other countries. Mother's Day is a new idea.

Being the youngest in the family, I am often overlooked, particularly in the department of family gift-giving.

The days get closer and closer to Mother's Day, and still no word from my brother and sister on ideas of what to do. I guess they think I know all about it. But how am I to know? I am too young to have pocket money. The responsibility slid past my left brain and ended up in the wild blue yonder of my imagination.

So I start to plot. Our house is still fairly new, and we—as a family—have been working every Saturday on getting the garden in shape. It is looking fine, except for the side of the house. It seems neglected, even half wild. My father puts up a trellis from the house to the fence. He plants a jasmine creeper on it, so that it will smell nice.

"I know what I'll give Mother," I think. "I'll trim the weeds that are underneath the jasmine and weave its long tendrils into patterns and form it into a wonderful sitting place for her. And I'll lead her out to it and offer to bring a chair out on hot days."

I spend days clearing the dead leaves away and rake the little square of green. I feel very happy.

The day before Mother's Day, my sister comes to me and says, "We've got a present for Mother tomorrow—and you are a part of it, too."

"What is it?" I ask.

"It's a vase for flowers," she replies. So that is that.

Mother's Day comes, and then it is done. I feel half glad and half sad. Mother loves her vase. I don't tell her about the sanctuary I had prepared.

I don't tell her for years. In fact, I never tell her. It is still my secret. It is still my longing.

Sit Back and They Come

It's a hot day in the Blue Mountains,
and you are alone in the bush,
sitting on a large sandstone rock
underneath a huge gum tree
which is shedding its bark in great strips
that hang loose from the bared branches . . .
for all the world like a naked lady
nonchalantly dangling a stole from her shoulders.

Only problem is, ants are walking in long lines up
and down the bare skin of the trunk. But the tickling
sensation which you almost feel as you watch
doesn't affect the hot stillness of the bark-stole.

Sit back, but how can you sit back in any
kind of comfort? Who could talk about stillness
in the bush? First and foremost, of course, is the
busyness of the ants. Then there are the insistent,
shrill whines of the cicadas . . . sounds that come in
both ears at the same time, so that the sound waves
crash inside your head when they meet.

And the birds. Well—one is never alone in the bush.
Get in the way of the ants and it's like walking
the wrong way in a railway entrance at rush hour.

Sit back where the Currawongs sit in the stunted
gum trees, up in the mountains.
They will swoop noisily past your ears warning
that you are the one who is trespassing.

Sit on the edge of a sandstone cliff
and the cockatoos will screech past you. . .
screech a warning that you
are violating their territory, and you'd better
watch out for them.

The Kookaburras will sometimes giggle
and then laugh hilariously.
The Galahs will pass noisily—
a gray and pink cloud disappearing overhead,
into the valley.

Only the largest animals remain quiet—
the silence of the Wallabies.

Robin

I stood on the edge of the playground . . . a student teacher calling the three-year-olds . . . it was time to go inside. They all came, except Robin, a large youngster who could be stubborn at times.

"Robin, I called you in. Did you hear?"

Robin glanced over her shoulder in my direction, but made no other move.

I got a bit angry and sharpened my voice a little more.

"Come on, Robin. I know you heard me."

For the second time, Robin ignored my words and remained immobile.

I walked over to her as she was standing on the broken section of the concrete path; I was increasingly curious.

"Robin, I've been calling you; it's time to go in for lunch."

She flung around, her face suffused red with a mixture of anger and determination.

"I'm not Robin. I'm Silver Mary Flower Gold."

Unbraided

"For heaven's sake. Just stay still long enough for me to get these tangles out!"

They were standing in the kitchen. On the end of the table was a hair brush, a comb, and two hair ribbons—navy blue. This was the morning ritual. After the ablutions, after the dressing in school uniform, after the piano practice, and after a quick breakfast—in silence with her father and brother — then came the brushing and combing and plaiting of the hair.

Then the rush out to the car and off to school, the hair problem forgotten for the rest of the day.

Except—yes, there were some problems. It was a nuisance to have to swing her plaits to the back of her head while she was playing vigorous games. Her hair would get caught in the branches as she climbed trees. Carrie recalled a holiday she had spent with one of her school friends. This was before her mother had taught her to plait her own hair. She had climbed pine trees, gone swimming, and rowed boats—for a week—without worrying over her hair. The tangles were almost insurmountable. Luckily, a friend of the family understood her dilemma and spent two hours combing out all the tangles.

"Yes," Carrie often thought, "I'd love to have short hair."

Sometimes, when she mentioned it out loud to her mother, the reply would come back.

"You know your father would not approve."

So Carrie put up with the inconvenience and the bother of combing out the tangles. Then, one morning, her mother suddenly said, "You know, your father is going away for a month. He has some business to attend to in the Northern Territory, so I thought we might go to a hairdresser and get some advice about your hair."

Carrie could hardly wait for the day to come. Finally, she and her mother walked into the local hairdresser's establishment. Carrie was fascinated. Everything seemed to be pink, white, gold, or silver. There were two lean-back chairs in the salon.

"Salon," thought Carrie, "what a wonderful word!"

"Carrie!" It was her mother calling. "This is Debbie." She

introduced the hairdresser. "She's going to check out your hair."

Carrie climbed into the chair, a large cloth was draped around her shoulders. The hairdresser swung the chair around, and for the first time, she saw herself reflected in a large mirror.

Debbie unbraided Carrie's plaits and combed out her hair.

"Oh, I see the problem! It's split ends."

"It's what?" Carrie's mother asked. Split ends. It makes the hair quite difficult to comb. Tangles, you know." Debbie glanced sideways at Carrie.

"Will it be like this all my life?" Carrie sounded skeptically scared of a future full of hair problems.

"The best thing is to keep it short," the hairdresser advised, "and then you won't have to deal with tangles all your life."

Carrie looked across the room to her mother, who was looking serious. Should she say something? Would she have to beg to get it cut? Would she have to wait for her father's approval?

She didn't have to wonder long. Her mother put Carrie's insecurities to rest.

"Well, I think perhaps we'd better have it cut."

And the hairdresser did just that.

Carrie watched happily as the long hair fell over her knees to the floor. Even her soul felt a whole lot lighter. She and her mother almost skipped home. But then . . . .

"What do you think father will say, when he gets home?"

"We'll face that when the time comes," her mother replied.

The days of apprehension passed by. Finally, the car came up the driveway. Carrie opened the garage door. Her father greeted her with his usual loving formality of a hug, and a remark:

"You're looking very beautiful tonight."

Naomi Louisa Mountjoy Long

Out of Whack!

He beat her when they got home drunk.
She bit his heel while he was down,
pulled off his shoe. Now,
he can't walk, uses a wheelchair,
which he loves to ride down hills.
He takes an umbrella with him sometimes—
puts it up and thinks he's flying!

She threw a canary at him once.
He thought it was a daffodil
and started crying.

No More Skirts

I wonder how women in the early days
of pioneering, in any country—America, Australia—
got around in those large, voluminous skirts.

How dirty they must have gotten.
What a tremendous amount of washing.
They didn't even have irons back then.

Before the days of girls wearing shorts in summer,
before the days of bare legs, even before the days of sneakers,
or what we Australians called sand shoes,

before the days of girls in slacks,
I spent holidays on a farm with my cousins and aunt and uncle.
Their son Keith was my buddy,

We were the same age—twelve.
Keith could move around so much more easily than I.
He had his trousers and shirt. I wrote home to Mother,

explained my dilemma about the problem with skirts.
Mother, even though a country girl, had grown up with skirts.
All that she could think to send me was a pair of riding britches,

or *jodhpurs* as we called them.
She must have felt a little self-conscious about sending overalls,
even though they would have been far more suitable.

Anything but skirts. I made do with the jodhpurs.
But fundamentally, I wanted to feel comfortable and happy.
I did not want to care what people thought.
Oh, for an old pair of overalls!

I Really Don't Know

I don't know how to use a computer,
and I don't know how to use a fax machine
or an adding machine.

I don't know who God is, or who the devil is,
or why they were invented. I don't know about
angels either, or why angel food cake is called
angel food cake. I don't know why vitamin C
is supposed to cure colds—or does it?
And I don't know why I don't get pneumonia.
I don't know what the minerals are that make
the rocks red and orange and yellow.
And I don't know how cars work.

I don't know how birds are able to sing
or whistle or whatever, and I don't know
how they understand each other—
and I don't know how they keep their feet warm.

I don't know why they're not putting bumper bars
on cars anymore, and I don't know what
we're having for lunch.

I really don't know.

The Lawn Was Still Green

for Aidan

The flowers were beautiful. The sun was shining.
My mother and sister had planned the flower garden
so that it would be ablaze with colour for my brother's
return. Purple stocks— their strong perfume—the blue-blue
of the lupines in their tall upright stance, and a border
of purple violets. The sun shone hotly. There was no breeze.
The lawn was still green; summer had not yet set in
to wilt and brown the grass.

Our housekeeper stood at the edge of the lawn,
where it met the concrete path, her hands clasped
under her apron. Peace with the Japanese. World War II
was over—and had been for a week or two;
why no news of my brother?

My father was away somewhere, officiating at a funeral—
someone in the parish had died—so mother was doing
her wishing prayers alone with the flowers.

A boy rode up through the gate, got off his bike
and walked over to me with a telegram.
I hesitated to take it—all during the war
these yellow telegrams had broken news of loss,
tragedy, sadness. Was this one of those?
Mother said, *Open it.*
I opened it and read the news.
Aidan had died two weeks before.

There was no breeze.
The lawn was still green.
All I could do was cry.

Driving into the Sun

I remember wishing
the sun wasn't so bright.
I remember someone saying
it's silly to live on the west side of the city.
You drive into the sun going to work
and again coming home.

The sun is burning hot—it's 117°.
We are holidaying in a cottage by the sea.
The butter melts in the ice box.
The sand burns our feet. We wear
our sandals down to the waves.

I go swimming with my Aunt Mabs.
It's fun—uncovered on the beach.
The sun burns me.
Big blisters rise on my back.
I sleep on my stomach for a month.

I go fishing with my friend
and her father.
The sun glares down on us all morning.
My knees are bare.
In one hour, they are a mass of little sun blisters.
I cry when I stand up.
I cry when I bend, then sit down.
I cry—I am homesick.

I remember wishing
the sun wouldn't burn like that.
I remember someone saying
it's silly to stay out in it all day.
I know now.
We need some shelter
in our lives.

Pacem's Memorial

I look at this great, loungy, black, curly dog.
He looks at me and we fall in love immediately.
Pacem is the friendliest dog.
He loves to ride in the car with me. He'll sit
up on the front seat and almost tell me where to go—
as if he knows.

He has one problem, though. He loves to bounce
his way through the woods, especially if he knows
I am going out somewhere where he can't go.
Call to him? No way! He'll run up on the hill,
look at me with bright eyes that say, *Hey you're*
calling me in, but I ain't coming.
Then I spend ages trying to catch him.

A friend of ours says, *You know, you can train him.*
Put him on the end of a long rope and if he doesn't
come freely when you call, pull him in.
So I go and find a long rope. Tie it on to his collar,
and we start running around. I throw a stick for him
to retrieve—which he does. Then I call, and he comes.

Great! I think. I'll try it again. And we go through this
routine without fault, four or five times.
Now! I think to myself, he should have the message.
I call; he brings the stick back, even if I don't pull
on the rope. So, I undo the rope, drop it to the ground,
and throw the stick.

He runs after it, picks it up. I call, expecting him to respond.
But Pacem is no fool. He knows the rope is not tied!
He bounces off into the woods. I can almost hear him laughing
as he tosses the stick into the air.

I Hear Myself Crying

I remember how it was with us.
Yes, I remember your smile, your greeting—fragile—
as you swept the hallway at the centre.
And I invited you to come and see Malcolm's play.
I seem to remember I invited you back to my apartment
after the show. Why am I not really sure about it?
You were so gentle—so loving.
And I invited you again—and you came again.
And I kept inviting and you kept coming.
You enjoyed my dog.
Remember how we used to take her for walks?
How she used to greet you—
her tail swinging back and forth.
You looked so beautiful together,
both of you slim, dark, smiling, smooth.
And then we returned.
The dog would be in the background
with her fur, and you were smooth—
smooth and brown and warm—
and your arms around me gave greater warmth
to your kisses.

Come, come—I hear myself crying to you now—*come*.
And you came then—softly—arms encircling
as we drew each other onto the bed.

Poking About

So maybe Russ will come. I really don't want to tidy up (either *the dome*—a classroom where I hang out—or my room). Yes, my conscience is full of shoulds, but I know if I go poking about in all my familiars, I will lose my sense of tidy direction—I will lose the straight road to the logical dignity of the mind. Oh, shit. Let me out.

My soul is stifled by papers and tools and other people's craft *stuff*, and my half-accomplished wood carvings and the old magazines I haven't read yet, and the books I've borrowed because I wanted to read them—and I haven't yet. Well, that's part of my stifled soul. There is more? Yes, there is more.

But let me clear out from this mess of *stuff*, get my walking stick, put on a jacket, and grab an apple. Away I go, into the realm of the birds, the woods, the farther fields, the pond. I'll take the path to the lake; wonder if it is still frozen.

The wind whips up to my jacket as I cross the bridge. I walk across this human-made structure—feel as if I'm on the arms of the apple trees as I near the other side. I look down, twenty feet or so below me; the scrubby bushes cushion the rocky surface of the earth.

I reach the end of the bridge. There is some wind for the windmill—whirring softly—it's a friendly noise for such an essential source of power. I wonder if we can use more wind power.

But on this day, who cares? Run free. No flowers out yet, but there are buds on the dogwoods—there are redwings around the swamp. The moss is greening bright and the chickadees pilot me around, and Hey, Ho—it's almost spring.

And What's in the Drawer?

The parrot belonged to the household, a mother, a father who disappeared every so often, and two girls—Daisy and Olive. Someone had given the girls that parrot. Sometimes the cats, and there were three of them, would try and coax the parrot into their eager claws, but always Daisy was there to free it from their possessive grasp. It was an ordinary green parrot—didn't do tricks, didn't even talk, but it did make lots of loud noises, as parrots do.

Daisy's and Olive's mother had to work. She cleaned people's houses and did their washing, so she was out every day and often did not get home again until after the girls were well and truly home waiting for her.

They were a churchy family and the mother became caught up in the fascination of the Second Coming of Jesus. There was a preacher around who had studied the whole of the Second Coming, and she would go to hear him. She would take the girls with her, to listen to the words of doom and gloom or hope and salvation.

That preacher had a tremendous pull in his sermons. He'd rant and rave about sin and how we would all be saved at the Second Coming. The pictures Daisy and Olive conjured up were magnificent—like people being caught up in the air as they went to meet Jesus, who would be floating around up there. In fact, once Daisy wanted to die to see what would really happen.

Then, the wonderful green parrot died. Daisy's's0 and Olive's mother thought the girls would have a burial ceremony—most little girls do that. So she didn't worry about the disposal duties. However, one day she began to notice a strange smell in the girls' room. At first she didn't take much notice, but several days later, it was a lot worse, so she investigated. She found the bird in one of Daisy's drawers.

She demanded to know what it was all about—this disintegrating parrot in a drawer full of clean good clothes. Daisy's reply was quite logical for a young lady. "Oh," she said, "he's waiting to be caught up with Jesus in the Second Coming."

Naomi Louisa Mountjoy Long

Recital

I'm in an old recital hall. There are some chairs around,
a piano against the wall with a large crucifix hanging there,
a cardboard box and a straw broom.

It's all neglected. It's there—waiting.
And there's no one around to warm up the keys.
It's far across the room.

There's all this space between myself and the piano . . .
will I ever be able to walk across that stage?
The whole audience watches, waits.

I hear the messy sounds of last-minute coughs
from the audience, the wretched squeak in my left shoe.
What if my period starts as I'm walking across the stage?

Will the piano bench be the right height?
My throat is dry—will it turn into a coughing fit
or just a tickle in the throat every second or so?

Does the piano have two or three pedals;
what if I press the one that dampens the sound?
God! Let me get through this piece okay—

I will never offer to perform again—oh, damn!
I forgot to take my ring off, and I would have to wear
my favorite silver one. It's really too big and hampers my playing.

Everybody's glaring at me. I can see in my mind's eye
a mixture of settled, self-satisfied, and prideful parents.
I see school friends rooting for me, but they can't shout it out—

not in this hall—the last minute clearing of throats —
my music teacher's wide, round eyes.

Sweet Shit

I step into the shower. It is cool;
it is comforting just to feel clean
in the way showers always
help me feel clean.

I remember, after swims
in the local baths and the hot
walk home, the nice cool shower.
Alone.
After a scorching day at school—
a nice cool shower.
After surfing or just playing around
on the beach—a nice cool shower.
Alone.
Nobody to worry about. It doesn't matter
whether my stomach sticks out, or I
have a roll of fat around where I
should have a nice slim waist—
or should I spell it waste?

All alone, I step into the cool spray
of the shower; I close the door,
and I don't even look in the mirror.
I let the cold water slide across my
shoulders—watch it cascade over my breasts—
funny shape, but what the hell—I'm the only
one here, and I'm not in a fashion show!
Watch out for the cold water
on my nipples—wow!

And the cascades tumble down my body,
through my fingers as they feel across
my stomach—yes it's too fat, but—oh well!

And what a wonderful trickling down my legs—
oh, the sensations—the joys of the little waterfalls
from my hips down to my feet!

I raise my face to the shower for its massage.
I'm lost in the cool wetness, and then—
Hey, Nom! Get the hell out of the shower . . .
Sweet Shit!

Driving Home

There is a grace
in older age—
a grace in bending down
to recover
a dropped pencil
a spilled coffee
a forgotten condiment
a lost word.

And it is beautiful
driving home from the store,
the sun at my back,
the moon a pale
luminous orb
ascending a light blue heaven.

We live long,
standing straight,
up from our feet.
It's our shadow
that lies on the road.

Hot-thighed Bride

Carol Cullar

Photo by Annie Rodgers

"Art's service is to the spirit, from which it removes the misery of inertia."
Louise Glück

Each individual creates a mythic self, a movie of her/his life in which s/he plays a starving role, but the lyric poet finds her/his *ego-ipseic* myth so magic, so compelling s/he is forced to share. I am a lyric poet: I want to provoke you, persuade you, penetrate you, please you. I want my texts to become flesh, your flesh. I want to play with words, make love to each image—not merely verbal onanism, but a gang-bang we can all get-off on. I want to feel the satisfaction of finding *le mot just*, weave the emotion, idea, image of my original thought with ever richer tapestry, see the event as an objectified reenactment that occasionally reveals the limited truth, and on rare occasions, the great. I want to elucidate each moment, imbue that moment's act with awareness, and in so doing, lift the humblest "squat" or "grunt" to highest art. I write for the moment in which the scattered fragments coalesce to become a sum greater than the parts, a vessel brimmed with mead—chill and quenching to the spirit's tongue.

I make a chart or grid. Vertically, on the left go nouns, along the top I place abstract categories such as: geographic, scientific, sociologic, historic, family, mechanical, political, global, personal, sexual, even meteorological—whatever I can think of at the time, but at least twelve or more (so that I am forced to dig and stretch). The goal, then, is to compose similes or metaphors for the noun relevant to the appropriate category. The most creative juxtapositions come after the page is full, and I randomly break apart the nouns and their original metaphors, creating new, and startlingly fresh expressions, which give rise to new texts.

Photo by Daryl Bright Andrews

Carol Cullar

Fire, Rain, and the Need to Act

before man, in the year <u>ome</u> <u>acatl</u> ° (two reed)

I.
the year after the world formed,
when things were simple, Mixcoatl,

the Cloud Serpent, made fire from sticks.
We are not told how many times he tried

and failed, nor if being Cloud Serpent and wind god
made this chore easier or not. It could be

that without fingers or even the thought
of fingers, this could be a tricky task;

it could be that time on time the flame
arose, the flapping cloak of Mixcoatl

would snuff each tender blaze, and this
great god discover his very heart run

counter to his quest. Perhaps he saw
the potential for destruction and his heart

wasn't in it; but perhaps
a naked woman came to him, her hands

and lips blue with cold, looked him long
in the eye, reached for the fastening of his cloak,

slipped it from his shoulders, wrapt herself
in its folds, lay down at the base of a great

mountain, and then, then, in his nakedness
Mixcoatl, who burned with need, had only to touch

the dry tinder with his flesh for flames to arise,
for the woman to feel the heat and open his own cloak

to him, arms wide, welcome him and his burning;
and that night man was made.

II.
I've asked around, and youths from other parts
don't know, but grandmothers from this desert

all ken the hanging snake, have taken daughters
and granddaughters to the side and told

what must be done. It is a woman's task:
you must be swift to act, sure in execution—

a stone or heavy stick, a single blow, sufficient,
then drape his body on the fence, *high as high*

may be, now mind! Then and only then
will Mixcoatl heed our pleas, yield

to our petition, gather blue-black cloak
across the sky and bless this place with rain.

III.
Let the men dance
the dance of worship,
build strong *atlatl* and dart,
drum and drink
themselves to stupor
on *maguey* juice;
let them parade their skill,
desport themselves
upon the playing fields,
but when the time comes,
and the need arises,
women act.

he's crossed the river

the local scandal rag has said
foul play is suspected;
they fetched his body
up from the river
below the black train-bridge
where it had snagged
on pilings half in,
half out of water;
he wore his blue jeans
about his ankles;
six stab wounds to the heart,
seven cuts to the liver,
and three throat slashes
where his life ran out;
two roses and a snake,
a girl's name and five
other tattoos on
unnamed body parts
adorn his corpse;
they hauled his puffy
four-day-dead remains
out the texas side
of the *rio grande*—
which must mean
that this is hell.

Relámpago°

When she was a child, a muddy child, in the mud-
caked streets of Cuidad Coahuila, she says they
broke *carrizo* poles beside the *arroyo* and with
those river canes touched that blue expanse
just above their heads. What woman would not
be shaped by this, knowing she had many times
touched the sky, and as a child?

But at times it goes the other way around—
de caelo tactus°° the Romans would have said.
First the blue gas and the torn crack, ions wash
the skin, cleanse the sacrifice: there is time for one
heartbeat crushing downward on lifeblood, thrusting
one more pulse toward extremities, then the caress
welds to earth the poised and muddy toe.

It is after the touching, when the clocks have all
been reset, the breaker switch thrown, the cat
dish emptied, that we go about our lives like
daughters on dark nights while mothers sleep,
after the gods pass, leaving only a stone.

°Spanish, *lightnin*
°°Latin, *lightning*
        literally, *touched by heaven)*

The Supplicant or The Bird Goddess Visits

She came to me, a pilgrim, pierced and panting, trailed by a silent
sidekick, (I never got the name, but the buns were nice, plexus taut,
eyes brooding.) Was I the individual to whom she spoke? Was I
the published poet? I said *yesss. . .* I was . . . I *am.* Call me *Battle
Stations* she said, (maybe she said *Panic Attack,* or it could have been
Epic Proportions, or *Cosmic Order).* And I knew she did not lie: the fuzzy
letters around the hollow of her throat announced as much
in the faded ink of old tattoos. (Hers was a long standing condition.)

She cut me off, got in my face; she roamed the house, pecked at all
my guests. She put an end to the feast and sneered at kitchen magnets
we assembled at our cozy klatch. She (wanted something from me)
inspected everything with curled lip, raised eyebrow; I saw the ratty
studio, tumbled foundations, and sagging walls, the clutter of my life
through her pale eye—so young, so lithe. She pointed out we'd both had
texts in *Restriction;* and as she perched to talk, her sidekick etched
the Celtic polychrome becoming her right calf; she ignored those
loving ministrations, intent on holding my attention.

I had guests I said. She had *need,* she said—(she'd come so far). And
did I think the nature of poetry rested with the poet or critic? I said I
have to be at work in twenty minutes; take your pierced titties and
brash act out of here. What makes you think you can interfere? I shoved
her out the door, watched her spiked hair coruscate against the setting
sun. She stalked, stiff-legged, through desert, (sidekick trotting one pace
back), and as she went, each feather she'd shed to set foot in my world as
mortal, bleeding woman grew back in flaming splendor; leg bones
thinned and lifted. I saw her beak had hardened as she turned to preen
a shoulder.

I'd lost the light; (the party'd spoiled), remembered my job was
temporary—they wouldn't call for me to sub at this late hour, knew I'd
never make the other side of Fort Worth in twenty minutes, anyway.
Not even the girl next door with the Lear jet in her garage could get me
there in time. I dithered on the threshold, yearned for Panic . . .

ran after to take on Epic Proportions. Knew I was about to disturb
Cosmic Order.

A Lenten Season

I.

He cuts asparagus grown too tall, too fast, works his nail up the stalk to
the still tender green—the precision point at which the living tissue is
again most vulnerable, snaps it off, lays it aside. Later the juices linger,
aromatic on age-dotted fingers caught in sunlight once too often,
too liver-kissed, nails ridged and stained with green; and the smell
is not the everyday urine-smell of old men's toilets, or at least the walls
and floors near those porcelain bowls, but that of onion or forgotten leeks
left too long, too late in dank refrigerator drawers, like flaccid penises
crimped in wheel-chaired laps beneath gnarled fingers that remember.

II.

Your refusal to cut me has left a sharp rejection under my tongue, as if
I were too mercuric, too volatile for your knife—yet I laid myself open,
endured your swift probes as essential indignities, preliminary rituals
to the robed ceremony. But you have said *no*, you will not open me
today, perhaps two weeks from now on a Thursday would be better.
Too busy, too protective of self, you will operate another day, leaving
this smooth aubergine to grow pendant beside red ovum, like Easter's
offerings forgotten on some back shelf in a faulty refrigerator.

III.

This Lenten season's bread leavens in hot Hispanic kitchens, wheels
of yellow-brown, plump with raisins, as each family dons new polyesters,
too tight, too bright, above scuffed shoes, shoes crimping knobbed
toes and cutting horned heels, ignored or beneath notice on the premise
that enough up top will compensate: enough hair, enough mascara,
enough cleavage, enough hip, enough knee and calf; and masses spring up
on odd days with ash on foreheads, either thumbed on by impatient
padres or scrolled arabesques that wear away in too much heat,
too little breeze through adobe chapels, whose bells toll absolution
or resurrection, as dusty shoes wend down cobbled lanes or scrunch
into '79 Chevys for the trip back to the house, where golden egg-loaves
bake, get broken, consumed, the extra stuffed into a spare *tienda* bag
and gravitated to the recesses of the fridge, as buds swell and spring
rites itself, and old women leave off corsets too small, too late to redeem
their missing loves or leftovers or lives.

Dumb Show

Oh, but you are wrong: the dead *do* lie to us, though I'm unsure
how I know this axiom will bear reflection: how their lips and eyes refuse
to meet our own, or their feet shuffle at the crucial moment—a small
dance-step of denial, how they refuse our overture, the wine and candy
calaveras° placed upon cold stones; but they are dead, and still
they shuffle,

> *only their hair and bone will not lie*

insist we buy their tale of stoppages or subways leading to frustration;
because they're so sincere, perhaps? The silence of their lips lies to us
in the shiny streets where moons fall into asphalt rivers of guilt, create
streaked paths of betrayal to our eyes, unpeopled by stars or
symphony; but they are dead and still refuse our ditties, stop their ears
with clay against apologies sung off key.

> *only their hair and bone will not lie*

Their patience dissembles in sullen rhetoric; prisoners of war,
they mime names and dates, leave us barren of their journey,
inconclusive of circumstance. Slim fingers feign acceptance, while
thin lips lie to us of hereafter;

> *only their hair and bone will not lie;*

yes, that must be our antiphon; these few scraps will endure to speak
a dumb show to us a thousand, five thousand years
from their lying down; and we will read of sex and age, birth/disease
and generation written there. Can any maxim lasting ten, or fifty
centuries lie? But then, you are right: the dead do *not* lie to us;
it is that we must listen slower to their dance.

° Spanish, *skulls*

Border Crossing

We're in line on the bridge—a broken string of mismatched pearls strung
across this skinny bottleneck of the Rio Grande; vehicles of pied origin

and destination, each rattletrap crammed with wants, spilling in Aztec
profusion from windows, thrust over tailgates like arms and legs

from the crowded interiors of wired-together '75 Chevys and
'83 Plymouths, wanting, watching the foot traffic going both ways faster

than our cars. We wait till a bored arm goes up, waving us onward
toward the barrier, our encounter with anomaly, the unfamiliar;

the truck in front farts out a cloud of unmuffled pollution, revs
into the space beside the armed guard as we inch forward. Rehearsing

our crude excuses, we watch for the unexpected, the crap-shoot
that determines *"revisión"* or *"pase,"* hope we will not be pulled aside

haphazard, and searched. There's always the mental check-list—will they
find some inadvertent contraband, some proscribed apparatus, anything

forgotten, forbidden? Will the mindless, blinking light let us through this
barrier into the foreign, the alien? Will we remember the words—*"vamos*

a hacer unas compras," ° or *"vamos a cenar"?*‡ What if the *aduana*†
asks us something philosophical or esoteric—outside our 500 word

smattering of pat phrases, something beyond our ken? Then the car
beside gets pulled over; two more in another lane pass through. We want

° Spanish, *"We're going shopping."*
‡ Spanish, *"We're going to eat supper."*
† Spanish, *customs official.*

their cheap liquor, the $5 bottles of tequila and Kahlúa, the antibiotics,
birth-control pills at one twelfth the price, the challenge of driving

with a different set of rules (that all-out bolt to be the biggest vehicle,
the first to the intersection), the daring to never look at the *other* (if you

look, you yield your right of way, concede another's right to the space
you wanted), each running under the premise of *"qui pega, paga"*—

"he who hits, pays"—so we jockey to be the front car, and Devil take
the hind-most. Now it's our turn to cross this barrier into the strange,

watch the random light of new technology strip decision from the guard,
rob him of his time-honored shakedown, award it to higher-ups, around

the corner. So we wait for green or red, *"pase"-"revisión,"* breath stuck
in our throats with exhaust fumes, guilt, anxiety, wants. We watch the

signal flash us through, free us to traffic with history and the mystery
of México, enter the third world, wend through throngs of *chicle* [°°]

vendors, every legless, twisted cripple that could be rented for the day
by beggars who've bribed officials for their special *lugarcita*. [††] But we are

not home free; the rules are all new. We've satisfied our mundane wants,
formed new hungers, thirsts, crossed the hindrance between our

understanding and our confusion; the real task lies ahead—if and when
we ever hope to return.

[°°] Spanish, *chewing gum.*
[††] *Spanish, small site*

Desiderata

Through the decades
dozens of gewgaws—
lost, misplaced, stolen—
fall through the net
of our perceptions
and are no more,
but in a dream
one night the *dueña*
in a dim *cantina*
came over to my table
and asked, *Do you recognize*
these vases? (There were three)
and on reflection
I said, well, yes,
I believe I do,
and she said,
You left them here
some time ago,
and are these
quilts and blankets yours?
Oh, yes! I recall
that those are mine.
They fell from the trunk
of your car as I followed
you to town one day —
and is that small husband
in the corner yours?
I said, One or Two?
And denied I'd ever
seen the man,
then *mariachis* came
to the table for a third round
of drinking songs.

Carol Cullar

The Serpent Asks, "Why Not?"°

I.

Because the second rainbow turns her skirts the other way,
a sibyl came for her and kissed her soundly on the lips;
at fifteen she discovers a moon on the tip of each finger,
strays content in foreign clime—Dryope wandering
through a star-dark night to pluck a single leaf
where lotus blossoms sway all thought
and each cartouche assumes a Nile of passion;
there scents of desert apricot delight
and restless tambours clack like river reeds
before a rising storm whose winds brush nipples
brought taut with chilling tongue,
while iron-hard bark creeps up her thighs
and sets the thrust of each toenail—deep, then deeper
in dark flesh, and
just before her ears are stopped
she hears earth-mother cry, *yes,*
and *yes!*   again.

II.

Andraemon, whose wood-wild lament wakens half the world,
who smells of sweat and lust; captures the furrows
of a hundred fields in eyes and skin with clouds
above his rising moons; those scars
from incidental nicks at seventeen
know each pyramid a hidden tomb, each branching
from the trunk a shoulder turned in mutability;
who runs too late to halt her deed
and in gnarled fingers can clutch but twig and leaf;
Ah, *Andraemon,* whose kiss on still warm bark and limbs
cannot set her free; who lifts his son
from nerveless hands grown green, and stepping back,
slack-jawed, cranes to watch her flower above him.

° Considered the most dangerous question. Robert Graves, *The White Goddess.*
° Dryope was punished by the gods for having plucked a leaf from a plant that in
actuality was another woman who had earlier incurred their displeasure; she was turned
into a tree and her husband left to raise their son alone.

Grace

I am kneeling
nude
on orange floral fabric,
head thrown back in melodrama—
blue lips, eyes closed,
shears
poised strategically in mid-air:
a large painting with childish
feet and tinker toys
deckled round the edge.

Don't marry him, Mother,
My daughter calls this latest masterpiece;
and so
I have hung such pubic splendor
here above my narrow bed where
none see—
to remind me of the wisdom
in most children's pleas.

But what
seamstress
having purchased such a bill
of soft goods
leaves her cloth untouched?
What fate, the thread uncut?

And what daughter,
seeing
her mother's frailties,
absolves in polychrome
munificence
with such a knowing hand?

Howie Wazatski

I hear my mother's voice—*don't we all?* Prosing on about getting some
perspective on my life, *making hay while the sun shines—the lord helps
those who help themselves—reap what you sow—lie down with dogs* . . .
and I thought of you, Howie Wazatski. You were number 5 or 6, I think,
the displaced Russian prince, or son, or grandson of a Russian prince
(does it ever end?), the Maseratti driver—the one after *Gary, Wilder, Paul,*
and *what's-his-name,* the cute one with dimples, ah, yes—and *Dave,*
and *Bob—*

What are you driving now, Howie? How big's your paunch, the bald
spot? How's it hangin' after thirty years? Do you still slap your girls
around; do you still call them *your* girl—slap 'em around a little to keep
them in line? Still pouring on the charm, lover boy? Tossing those lost
millions, the hidden rubies, your grandmother's, or was it your great-
grandmother's, flight to Paris into the evening's conversation over
candlelight and cheap wine?

Remember the one that got away—when it *all* got away from you?
That time in the mirrored bathroom—we were both drunk on vodka
and you tore my blouse, came on strong with some macho crap about
doin' things *your* way, slapped me silly; and I went out of body, laughing
—laughing for ten minutes at the dozens and dozens of angry men
that looked like you—the Russian prince in exile in a Byronic snit, black
curls falling onto theatric brow—and the thousands of me that swung
back in an arc into the distance, reverberating through centuries
and dimensions, in every lifetime asking to be victim—

Torn dress, bloody lip, swelling eye; and I laughed, hilariously,
hysterically, because I knew, ultimately, irrevocably, that I owned you
with pale puckered nipples on big breasts, and a pussy that wouldn't quit
—I already *had* what you wanted—it was *all mine*.

Remember, Howie, what price I paid for my freedom,
the independence to use you like Kleenex, toss you away when you got
limp, learn one rule: *do unto others, but do it first?* You taught me that
—so I remember your name, Howie Wazatski, when all the other tissues
that came after have gotten their numbers jumbled up and slipped off
through the mirror to other dimensions.

Then mother's voice chimes in again, *didn't you love any nice guys?*
I answer without thinking, *why on earth would I do a thing like that?*

The Alaska Question

What kind of man stands guard at the foot of Denali for two weeks with his bear gun, while on hands and knees I photograph tundra, then reads sex magazines till summer sun sets over the Big Susitna and all night in winter, then is too shy to come-on to me unless I put my hand on his crotch and blow in his ear?

What kind of man calls me from High Lakes when it's fifty below to tell me the Arctic fox ate from his hand again, and that as we speak, the aurora swirls above him in green fire, and another time when he crushes his leg under the snow machine a half mile from the lodge and crawls back to call and ask what kind of first aid he should try, while I stand helpless 7000 miles away in the Chihuahua Desert?

What kind of man convinces me to take flying lessons and buy a long barrel, Reuger .44 magnum, then when I qualify for my single engine land license, and from 30 yards out pop a tighter cluster with *his* 30.06 than he can, invites me to warm his furs forever?

I guess you weren't that kind.

Carol Cullar

Peace Sleep with Her

"Nor shall this peace sleep with her; but as when the bird of wonder dies. . ."
Shakespeare, *Henry VIII*

That's what happens in a two- or-three-horse
town: things grow organic, and cow-trails become
streets, throw off the imposition of Roman roads,
run higgledy-piggledy like lives branching off the geometric
or the flight of crows at dawn, all tilted from the ecliptic
with a five-degree moon vanishing before the orb of sun
can make sweet voice known in traffic or bird song,
the Cheshire-cat smile of said moon growing fainter
by the moment, deserting two planets, that at first caw of crow
succumb to day's advance; and those two or three horses
switch from restless hip to restless hip, nicker
to the morn at large, expect their hay soon and wonder
about dandelions in the south pasture as the first hint
of coffee and molasses wafts down the hill past chicken house
and budding rose. Volunteer firemen slop hogs and
open hardware stores; and Beverly at the all-night truck stop
hands her apron to the day-shift girl, wonders how her kids
got on with Jimmy Jack last night, shifts restless hips, rubs her back,
then stops off for milk and eggs at the "66" on her way home,
beneath unseen flights of crows, drives vacant-eyed
down those angled streets that run a little canted from the true.

Carol Cullar

last night over

margaritas at Moderno's
Mickey told me
that back at the end
of September he thinks
he might have had sex
with a DEA agent who
worked undercover at the
hospital, but since he
heard from a friend of hers
she had received death
threats in October and
left town the next day,
he has no way of knowing.
He thinks her name was
Cynthia, at least, that's
what she told him at the party,
or it could have been
Justine, but he's a little
worried because he only
remembers her naked,
astride with those funny
chins an older woman
gets when you see her
face hanging over you,
then there's the fact that
he woke up naked in
Mike's spare bedroom
about eleven the next morning.
Anyway, he's finally joined
the rest of us plagued with
those vague notions that
there could be another reality
swimming just beyond our ken,
so I made some soothing
sounds and reminded myself
to pick up a jug of milk
on the way back out of town—
saves a trip, you know.

What Fat Women Know

We know those skinny women hate us because they know in the marrow of their bony thighs every ounce of our rippling independence mocks the self-imposed tyranny of their frail flesh.

We know that lust is more vital and consuming, richer on the tongue than denial (to what end?).

We know that passion and satisfaction are two sides of the same coin in a very heavy purse whose richness will forever be denied the lean.

We know the eminence of *I*, the dead weight of *they*, having assessed at a gut level the strictures and conventions of this sick society and, upon the courage of our convictions, rejected the most blatant insanity that twists to its own ends the reflection in each and every girl-child's mirror.

We know the pleasure of excess, the excruciating delight of *La Religieuse* from any *patisserie* in Paris or Grasse or Antibes on a summer's day, the creamed ecstasy of *las ranitas* from that little bakery in the *Distrito Federal*, México, their pink stuffed mouths opened in supplication, their merry, chocolate eyes buried in green, honeyed flesh, laughing, begging *"eat me! eat me!"* and the fulfillment of doing so—with Cappuccino or Espresso on the side—two or three, if we choose.

We know beneath our ponderous breasts in muscular hearts grown thick and tough our mothers have never loved us, and nothing we will ever do, or not, can change that fact.

The Sound of Gravid

With all those concomitant implications of
grave and gravity, weight and mass, the belly-
roundness of the fact—fertility without
the euphemistic flutter of *enceinte*° (as in,
my dear, didn't you know? she's enceinte) and
the furtiveness of pregnant. (*got herself pregnant,
she did, knocked up her first time out!*) And
pregnant calls up images of poked, from the French
prenant, having been taken, willing or not—
an alien growth implanted, or the tendrils
of some mutating cyst wrapped about one's life
:to be expelled, adopted out, forgotten;
while *gravid* harbors within—a natural state—
the potential for perpetual fecundity,
recurring. Cows in daisied fields, lowing,
gravid in the sun, amber bellies
slick with morning dew or birdsong,
any bull but a vague half-memory
of other pastures, *then*. But now,
swiping rough tongue over the product
of their labors, munching away
at afterbirth—the only flesh they eat,
their own.

° French, *pregnant*

Carol Cullar

dies mellior‡

"donec gratus eram tibi" ° Horace

tattooed like a distant tropic
on turquoise reaches of the mind
woman-daughter climbs the metronome
of heartbeat, her soft fingers smudged
with bitter chocolate, *jumelle mienne,*†
her half-smile for my eyes alone
at two, at twelve, at twenty-two.
Smell of rain and earth and woodsmoke
in her hair; with phone calls
from odd toll booths: Monaco
across from the palace,
a roadside park out from Paris,
off Cornmarket Square, Oxford,
the nude beach beneath Golden Gate.
Hello, guess where I am?
I was here and thought of you—
had to call. I'm glad you're home.
So I am *Home*, as she is *Solace*—
tattooed like a distant tropic
on this earth spinning round
a molten core.

‡Latin, *better days*
°Latin, *"in the days when I was dear to you"*
† French, *my own twin*

Eulogy In White

How could I write of snow,
tell of cold and silent
purity in this place? Here,
where each agent conspires to thwart
its coming, where the earth is
a tan biscuit steaming, and
the river's waters leak slowly
down its beefy sides like thin
brown gravy, where is the place
for snow in such fractaled
chaos of burning dust?
This debauched Virgin reeling
as she stumbles her long way home
need never fear the frozen ditch;
this hot-thighed bride garbed
in dark mesquite will never wear
its whiteness to her marriage bed,
nor will all enveloping forgiveness
grace this brown *Jesus*: they have assured
their resurrection by other means
and will not be touched
by cold white fingers.
How could I write of snow?

Welcome Home Illusion

Margo LaGattuta

Photo by Bill Shippey

Pretending to be a Barn

Here I sit, alone in a field
pretending to be a barn. I hold
myself so still the cows could walk
right through me. Silence plants
my feet in deep, my heart deeper
than weathered wood. My eyes
like old glass windows, dusted
with lost days, are ready to hold
the new light.

        If a duck walked in,
he wouldn't find me here.
Or chickens circling and
pecking the ground. Even the wind
can't see me. My doors flap
and let anything in.

*In my poems,
I try to create an
explosion in the
senses through a
play between image
and sound. I love
unexpected word
combinations, the
way language can
transcend time.
Poems are alive and
happen new for each
reader. They change
to fit the ears and the
heart.*

Looking at life through the eyes of metaphor
(a creative comparison of two seemingly dissimilar things)
can be powerful. When you become a barn, for example,
all boundaries between yourself and barn begin to blur, and
you'll discover many common threads. Write a poem about
yourself as a particular barn (tree, lake, shoe, etc.) What
size and shape are you? Where were you built? How do you
experience your days and nights? What do you love and/or
hate about your life as a barn? Explore all possibilities — your inner life, your
celebrations and regrets.

Photo by Daryl Bright Andrews

Alone in America

I am fourteen and take the Woodward Avenue
bus to shop at downtown Hudson's. I count
my money, one hundred-fifty-six dollars
and twenty-three cents. I am amazed and
proud to be all grown up, like a fresh
avocado, ripe and ready for anything.

I could be anywhere this 12th of December,
1956, in Cairo or New Guinea, but I am here
on a Detroit bus by myself, a teen with hormones
that surge like Greyhounds through my radiant veins.

The bus driver eyes me like a hungry snake, as I
pull up my straight khaki skirt to board. I imagine
he is Jimmy Dean and misunderstood. I want to rebel
and drive a wild Porsche like Jimmy did, but I am now
becoming a young lady with white gloves and a veiled
pill box hat. I can buy my parents anything with this
pile of money in my alligator bag.

Money and wheels — the combination makes me shiver.
I'm so proud to be alive and alone in America, and
the riots in the streets won't start for years.

Looking for Elvis in Kalamazoo

He's been spotted in the Maypole
Diner, sipping coffee with the regulars.
He wears white socks and penny loafers,
stone-washed jeans and a button-down.

Elvis has gone real on us.
He might be anyone now.
He's discovered oat bran and thrown away
his sequins for a cotton blend.

Elvis is hiding in the Burger King,
playing chess with someone's grampa.
He doesn't even win sometimes.
He wants to be plainer than a fish sandwich.

Hordes of women in their forties
prowl the streets with their eyes peeled.
They've traced him with divining rods
to the front lobby of the Harris Hotel.

Hiking up their Underalls,
they dream of one last look at a star.
They watch the lips of the aging bell boys
for that famous quiver, that stray curl.

They know Elvis can't hide forever
under plain wraps in Kalamazoo.
Any moment now he'll slip out
and shiver in his ordinary pants.

Telling Stories

Margo LaGattuta

I am wolf woman.
Out of my green eyes
flow the Arctic winds
to spin and whistle
a tale for you.

First the halted howl,
then a tree dance enters,
and the story the tree tells
begins to tell me its versions.

And the mountains come running.
And all the wolves halfway
up the mountains come running,
and the few who are halfway down.

And there is a moon story now.
The moon is telling it slow
like a raw onion peeling back
layers of story and story.

And watch my wolf ways.
Watch me exaggerate and hear
the tempo rush through us,
a blackbird flutter in the heart.

Hear the bird story itself to us,
make a home in the bone
where every story wants to be held,
where every old story is breathing.

A black bird wants to fly
right in the eye of the wolf story.
And the long sky opens
to swallow the tale whole.

The Dream Givers

The dream givers live up there in the woodwork.
They are little people with eyes that can see
through walls. As a child, I knew them by
the shadows they left as they scurried under
my bed or in to my closet when I entered the room.

My sister, Susan, knew I had too many on my
side of the room we shared, so she snuck around
and piled some of mine up under her pillow. *Don't
worry*, she said. *When I grow up, I won't do this.*

The dream givers knew what I was looking for.
They waited in the attic insulation to entice me.
They wanted me to fall through the ceiling, like
my mother warned me about. And I knew I had to
fall through some day, into that other place.

Sometimes they still pull on my toes when I'm sleeping,
and the man I'm sleeping with scratches his nose. They
run all over his body, trying to wiggle their way in.
If he's dreaming about the sea, they bring their life jackets

and bob around on the waves of his slow breathing.
Nothing happens that they can't enter. Even
when I'm cutting cantaloupe, they sit perched
on the knife, and the fruit ripens with their singing.

Once Garin called them my prisoners, said I should
take them everywhere and force them to listen to my stories.
He asked where he could go to get his own set of prisoners.

But the dream givers can't be contained that way.
They fly around and snarl if I try to trap them.
Every new dream comes wrapped in their breath,
and none of the old dreams die without their mourning.

Briefly, in the Garden

I am the woman, alone with a white cat.
I am the woman with the long, old arms
that reach all the way back,
briefly, in the garden
to a life before this one,
to a dark-haired man who ate
pasta with broccoli, who ate
ripe tomatoes with basil and oil,
and my heart.

I am the woman who buried him
with his money in a very old chair
in a dream of our babies walking about
in his glass of Johnny Walker Red.

I am the one who lived to tell it.
I am the one who knows the bare facts
that he stuffed into his distressed leather valise,
into his crisp Armani suit and swallowed.

I am the wooden shelves he built to contain me.
I am the attic full of bats in this house of our dreams.
I am my sons' continuous sorrow.
I am the ragweed growing wild where he
once grew zucchini and summer squash to feed us.
I am the piles of paper he fed me in court.

I am the trips around the world he took to forget me.
I am New Guinea and Paris and Costa Rica in the sun.
I am the many Margaritas he chugged in London
and the sad young wife he married in Nevada —
married and left in eight months with her sable coat.
I am her hurt wail on his voice mail and her mother's tears.
I am the years before he turned his heart to ricotta cheese.

I am the woman, alone with a white cat,
the woman whose children have all grown
and moved with their stereos to Chicago.
I plant my garden of eggplants and violets and brief
good-byes that grow ripe on the tongue.

I am the woman with a white cat
who sees the past through
two different colored eyes.
One green eye for seeing darkness, one
blue eye for catching light.

Fish on Shaved Ice

gazing straight and still
in the market stall,
how flat your eye
is on me.
What caught you
with a hook in your plans?
You moved toward
some hope with your
bubbling hunger,
a bit of greed on
your parted lips.
A net
pulled you in,
startled, to lie
under glass, that
final hunger frozen
on your expectant face.

Soft Families

Lost in the dark moss
in the labyrinth of the hills
are the days I let you
touch me softly in deep
places I did not own.

Lost in the final fusion
of my heart to its memories
are your dark eyes, your granular
hands on my periphery, my will.

Our children have been digging
in the gardens of various states.
They've been pulling up roots
and earthworms in their searching.

Our children have been watching
the old films of their innocence,
piecing together the shards of a life
we all shared in a suburb.

It is morning again, and the sun
arcs through my window, mimics
the shattered spray of electric
memories that will not cohere.

It is morning in America, and hordes
of our children are digging. Hordes
of our children are asking for promises,
for pieces of our hearts for breakfast.

It is too late for sausage or French
toast in America, where our children
are begging to feed on us, where
the menus are full of fried custodies.

Families are grimly separated
at church picnics or on washdays
when they least expect it, and loss
seeps in like jam on a soft slice of bread.

There are choices, and men and women
in America have been wild in their solitudes,
and it is too late for regrets, it is too late
to be insular and cry behind doors.

Lost in the dark moss
in the labyrinth of the families
are our reasons for breaking down
in the soft frenzies of our hearts.

Margo LaGattuta

Wearing the Jewels from Korea

for Mr. and Mrs. Bae

My amethyst and ruby ring has traveled
far, over distant continents and oceans
to land here, where it fits perfectly,
on my ring finger in Rochester, Michigan.

I wear its red fire, a stone I know
has come to me through great love
from the family of my son's new wife.
It was chosen by a gentle Korean mother
whose third finger matches my own.

We give each other our delicate jewels,
hers a shining daughter with deepest eyes,
mine a magical son with inner glowing,
and we spin a ring of families.

A wedding of souls, of distant
customs and unfamiliar words,
has made a link through time.
It shrinks the complicated world
to the size of a jewel in our hands.

My new relatives and I speak
in different tongues, yet our eyes
share a language of the heart.
We give each other precious offspring,
our irreplaceable jewels, to love.

Margo LaGattuta

Ultra Sounds

for Shanie and Mark

The sound of my granddaughter
is soft on shining paper,
metal gray shavings like a face,
like eyes, yes, I see eyes,
the sound of eyes coming at me.
She lifts arm to forehead
with a sound like waving,
like a first wave. I think
it's her forehead. Isn't
that my nose? She is too
new riding earthward on a
sound in that pink cradle.

I remember her father, a curving
fetus in my own young womb
thirty years ago in Germany.
I remember the tickle of his hands
long before pictures of sounds of hands
were ever possible. I saw him
once in a dream, his pre-formed hands
entered my mind on a silver sound
one 3:00 AM when I couldn't sleep.
A gift without paper, his eyes
moved through night sounds
to stare at me, his body still
on the other side of being.

Laminate, my daughter-in-law says.
I want to keep this picture forever.
So we put it through, cook it in plastic
and out it comes, all black and indistinct
from the heat. Some ultra sounds
can't be contained. The heat
of too much knowing
and holding on . . . burns everything.

Margo LaGattuta

Remortgaging My House

All living is on the wire; all else is waiting. Papa Wallenda
is setting myself up for uncertain
numbers and how they can float,
can hover in my brain that must decide
exactly what to choose, like in a dream
where the rearrangement of internal time
and flying percentages makes logical sense.

My broker says it is important to sense
the acceptance of fixed uncertainty
and reminds me that in one year's time
my 5 3/4% interest rate could easily float
in either direction, up or down, as in that dream
where I am one of *The Flying Wallendas* and must decide

the pros and cons of personal gravity. How can I decide
if my own flexible outlook on love makes sense
when any day my interest can go up or down, my dreams
can show me plunging below to the waiting net, uncertain
of whether I will hit rock bottom or float
up, escalate over the trapeze to a place where time

isn't an unknown at all, where (inside the heart) time
always moves at a fixed rate, regardless of decisions
I make, or whether I'm having adjustable fun? My 2% can float,
depending on some national or global occurrence. What sense
does that make? I never seem to be quite certain,
like the rate of my escalating mortgage, whether to count on dreams.

Once my house was high on stilts in a dream,
and there was a liquid silver clock, making me gasp as time
stood still. The cement foundation was gone, creating uncertainty
and panic about what to trust. I had to quickly decide
which way to flee before my official deeds and senses
became water-logged when the house began to float.

This is how my new mortgage can float,
my prime rate hopefully dropping 2%. I dream
of my flexible bank account finally making sense.
Maybe even love will make sense sometime,
and I won't have to toss a coin to decide
whether my heart is adjustable or still uncertain.

A sensible mortgage of the heart takes time.
Any interest or hope can float up or down. Any dream
can decide to escalate, if one embraces the uncertain.

Linen

It is nice to have
straight towels,
I suppose.

When the truth emerges
you will be prepared if
your towels are arranged
by color
in the right rows
in your closet.

One day
it will all make sense
when the Laundry Inspector comes
to examine your life.

He will nod his approval
at the whiteness
of your washcloths.
His eyes will sparkle
if your fluff still holds.
He will look it all over
make notes, smile shyly,
and present awards
for folding.

My Welcome Home Illusion

for Adam

It is your magic show,
my son, holding this day
in your hand like a rubber ball.
Yesterday is another red ball

on the table,
covered with a plastic cup.
Abracadabra, you say,
moving time around,

watch my hands, Mother.
And I wonder how you know this.
Today is your welcome home illusion,
you say. My eyes open to it.

I watch the balls vanish
into air, the plastic cups
empty themselves.
It's a winter afternoon.

You wave your silk scarves
at me, and the balls
multiply, then cups, then
tables and years.

I see you
in the middle of your act.
Now you trick me.
Now you don't.

On My Birthday, Bats

Margo LaGattuta

barge into my quiet room. They hang
high on the rafters of my sloping
bedroom wall. Out of all the hideouts
in Oakland County, flying bats pick me,

dive-bomb my bed at dusk;
their radar tunes in. Their
wings stretch to gracefully glide
over my dreams, my curled
inner world. I hear
their high-pitched squeals
as I fly right out of my skin
and down the hall to crouch
down into the dark corners of my
sleeping self, my night crashes
in waves of shock and invasion.

Now the bats enter my sleeping poem.
I am older; I am growing wings.
The poem wants to fly through my
window, singe the air with its
radar beams, its high-pitched sounds.

The poem sleeps in the woodwork
by day, and by night it bats
over my head, flying low syllables
in my ear. It wants to soar
through the ceiling and out

my open kitchen door into your
chimney or the hole in your roof.
The poem wants to catch you
unaware, wants to stick to your
face and be your friend.

You'd better not duck; it's
my birthday, and I'm sending bats.

Light Support

Out of the night, jagged
images of pantyhose, mouse-
gray, cinnamon and taupe,
lie gnarled and twisted
in my diaphanous dream drawer,

like they've been caught trying
to run somewhere and gotten
a case of the jitters. I see
myself pulling them on,
looking for one clean pair,
coaxing them over bare legs
only to find rips and holes.

Each window in the broken mesh
punctuates my dream, my life,
my tangled stretch support.
Each yank and tug is a hope —
sheer black, sheer nonsense,
giving way to control, to power.

I feel my medium-to-tall Wonder
Legs in fashion colors flap
under me as I pull myself up
like a sandalfoot queen
rising from the nylon night.

Cleaning Rooms for My Mother

It is time to clean house because
my mother is coming. She'll be here
in early June. When I see her again,
my mind will travel from clean rooms
and dark night fevers to the day she cut
the tip of her index finger off, peeling
potatoes. The blood on the table

is still red in my mind forty years
later as I write it. My fingers are falling
asleep on the keyboard. The forsythia
bushes look especially luscious this year.

I remember finding the slice of her skin
on the kitchen table the next day. I was
really hot, and my fingers, my heart
were thick with worry. Will she know
what it means if I tell her now on a
whim, or will she still say, *I love it when
you write those happy poems, Margo*.

Stopping for a Bite

Margo LaGattuta

In a truck stop diner in Indiana
I hear the news. The Gulf
War is now a real war,
and I order a grilled
chicken sandwich deluxe
(hold the mayo) near Gary, Indiana,
on my way home to Michigan.

I stare at the all-I-can-eat salad bar,
fresher than most, with cherry
tomatoes and alfalfa sprouts,
a tray of unsalted sunflower seeds.

Strangely, there are pay phones
at each table. *In case a war
breaks out,* I think, *and I must
call my sister in Connecticut.*

So I do. *Hello, Susan,*
I say. *This is the first war
I can remember as clear as endive
and a pile of grated cheddar.
How are you? I feel afraid.*

I could be anywhere this
tin-type night. I could be home
watching Ted Koppel explain attacks
on TV. I could have a brother on the
front or see action myself. But no,

this sinking feeling in Indiana
tossed with vinegar and oil
is sprayed with violence,
and I am alone with seven truckers
trying to decide between the house
dressing and the raspberry vinaigrette.

Margo LaGattuta

The Wish Bracelet

The way to love anything is to realize
that it might be lost.   Fortune Cookie

They say you tie it on your wrist
and wear it every minute,
even in the shower, or in a hurricane,
or in bed with your lover.

Mine is purple, green and orange
and came from Guatamala.
Mine is the color of joy,
the power of wishes tied in knots.

They say your dreams come true
the day the bracelet falls off.
My arm is heavy with the burden.
I carry the gift of loss around me.

I carry the gift of waiting
for small threads to fray,
for each color to begin bleeding,
for the friction dance on my skin.

To know wild colors now
is all hope in a circle.
Anything beautiful might be lost; I see
everything real keeps moving.

Margo LaGattuta

Bridge of Birds

The day was counting up its birds
and never got the answer right.
Unknown

As you enter the day
remember to walk lightly
on their wings, the fluttering
arc across sky shifts
with each weightless step.

If you follow the singing,
a wild bridge calls
you high over Lake Superior
and you count on this,
each bird a gray memory
moving under your fast feet.

Three mourning doves
wake you and multiply,
squaring off to the ninth power
between your startled eye
and the next floating thought.

Grounding yourself in birds
will be your first miracle.
After that, all numbers grow teeth,
and your life, a bridge of birds,
becomes divisible by trees.

Breathe Through Your Nose

Shanda Hansma Blue

I write to explain the world to myself, to work out an understanding of the events of life in the physical and political world. That is not to say that I write a precise autobiography! Rather, this is life cannibalized for art. It is an appreciated side-effect if what I write also applies to others—the specific becomes universal.

I owe my participation in this project to the English Department of Western Michigan University, the George Baker Scholarship, and the philanthropy of Mr. James Easterly Walker of Barberville, KY. and Kalamazoo, MI. I sincerely thank all of them.

I dedicate this work to my children, Danyi Hansma Heckaman, Morgan Genevieve Blue, and Graydon Courtney Blue.

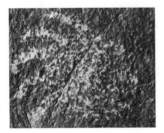

Have a friend or fellow writer make a list of eighty or more short phrase and one-word prompts such as; "your home town, an ugly color, a fruit, a foreign city," etc. Then write your immediate responses in a list; use as many of them as you like, or can, to make a poem. See my poem ". . . ass Avenue" as an example of the results. The poem and/or the story is in the physical details.

The Maple Wood

was deep green until
nights of chill breeze
set the trees a feverish flush.
I thought they could recover
but the weather grew colder
and their complexions turned
to a blush which bled
drop by drop to the ground
until a steady rain left
a large red stain beneath
skeletons whose limbs
I could hear clattering,
summoning all souls,
proclaiming all saints,
until children came
to demand their tithe.

On the Love of Reindeer

When I decided to become a reindeer
my feet wanted to cleave into hooves,
my head yearned to sprout
an intricate rack of antlers.
I wanted to feel the butt and nuzzle
of a small furred head at my side,
my breasts needed to suckle a calf.
I began to keep company with a wolf
who knew my thoughts and could sense
the pastures to which I wandered
grazing the green mosses and lichens
found under the snow
which was my beverage, cold and clean.
All the various cells of my body
replacing themselves in the natural
process began to replicate every iota
of the reindeer I loved each day.
The reindeer in me remained concealed,
pretending to be a woman. Sometimes
in my appearance others would remark
on the proud carriage of my head,
the strength of my stance,
my nimbleness on difficult terrain.
My heart grew to the capacity of the tundra,
my brain encompassed the nature
of my new world,
awakened to the warm gush of the milk
of the mammal hearing the bawl of her young.
When I loved a man he tasted the moss
of the cool tundra in the warmth
and sweetness of bee stings from my breasts.

Angle of Refraction

*(ca 1737)-the angle
between a refracted ray and the normal
drawn at the point of incidence to the
interface at which refraction occurs.*

Everything that flies is not an airplane
but many things must keep their noses up to remain airborne
so we are lying on our backs letting the blue make us dizzy
like the effect of jazz and booze in a smoke-filled room.
We watch the bellies of planes as they leave the earth,
roaring, a few yards before they reach us. This is scary science.
Viewed through the grass beside the runway the tar shimmers
in reflected pools of sun. He says he's trying to decide on an approach.
I say, *Get clearance from the tower? Full flaps and reverse throttle?*
So many ushers have given me so many directions I am not sure
whether I am at the wedding or the movie.
Is this a life? A landing?

*Or a change in the apparent position of a celestial body
due to bending of the light rays emanating from it
as they pass through the atmosphere?*

Everything that flies is not lighter than air but almost any
atmosphere is thinner than the smoke in this airport lounge.
These are the flat notes not written in the score which turn a classic piece
to jazz and this is the sharp note improvised in the "Lullaby of Birdland"
that turns all the birds' songs blue.

*Or the action of distorting an image by viewing it
through a medium?*

People fly for their own reasons. Like the bend of a ray of light
when it passes from air into glass, translated from wave to particle,
one medium into another, music moving motes,
comets passing planets circumnavigating stars, art, practicing

Allegretto in F from *"Eine Kleine Nachtmusic."* Was "a little night music"
a euphemism for love-making before Mozart named this piece, or after?
Is it a coincidence that the Scottish National Symphony likes to play
Prokofiev's Suite from "The Stone Flower" with its opening fanfare
of brass echoing the sound of bagpipes?

Could forces combine, orbit each other
like the twin stars of Alpha Centauri,
make twice the light and heat?
I meet his gaze in the haze
of the airport bar. *"Contact."*
Is this an interface? A take-off?
Flight?

Slots

I sense that, for you,
this apartment is like
being in a hotel mid-day,
more cars than you expect
in the parking lot.
A kind of gambling establishment,
the throb and pulse of many bodies.

This place is jumping.
Terra cotta pots on the balconies
leap to the ground,
geraniums take a leave, go awol,
are at liberty anyway.

Strings of lights left from the holidays
swing, jive, as dusk comes
but are calm as they reveal
your ardent face, restless body
exit to supper hour.

What can I cook for you?
Just hours ago in this place
I was eating oatmeal, taking
a chance conversing with you
when head, heart, and hormones
lined up like three stars
in a clear night sky,

assembled themselves in a row
like the fruit of a one-armed-bandit
spilling cherries in my arms.

Rhythm

On being invited to manufacture
love with the dead man I am surprised
but he is so disarming as to be awful
and effective. We are between sheets
before I have time to deliberate. His kiss
and his body are enthusiastic.
The dead man says he devours the bodies
of women younger than he,
which is all of us. I have become
one of an uncomfortable crowd.

I am allowed to caress the dead man,
his body is harder than I expect
and his hair longer and thinner.
He shivers as my hands glide his sides.

The dead man says he could do this forever.
I think of this as not so idle boasting
but very like a man, living or dead,
and I don't want to find out
being accustomed to a live man.

The dead man wants to do tricks, I don't.
I want to make love with him like an old
married couple, thinking he is as familiar
in my life as I am in his,
but he has a foreign rhythm,
we are not synchronized.

The dead man does not whisper poetic phrases
in his progress to ecstasy. He yells
Faster, Faster! and holds my hips
moving me harder. When he comes
his limbs thrash like a tree in a tornado,
and I pray he will survive this act
which I hope is not just for my benefit.

$E = MC^2$

Reading too much in a week-end (drowning asphyxiation by H2O,
water, a mix, elemental chemistry [How can we cool the cooling towers?
Where store the waste? How long?]) I surface wondering which book also
has a one-shoed man in it, or is it multi-display large screen television?
Don't call on a cellular phone. This is a private conversation.
Does biology = telephone? Is it like any other team
we could field in our favor?

As a child I could only wish atoms had not split, been smashed
when jets cracked our windows, learned to fly faster than sound,
dropped practice bombs called "shapes" as if they were an innocent cure
like *blanc mange*, calf's-foot jelly, or some other molded gelatin to soothe
the wire nerves of the universal mechanism on its way to a super-collision
during math anxiety when improper fractions were just
more ill-mannered numerals while my systolic/diastolic surge
like the tide, ripened.

DNA's high-tech hieroglyphics in all these tenuous lives' events
add up to *deja-vu* or not quite. Details differing in space or time.
How long can we continue to listen for order in chaos?
Physical scientists trying to decode what poet philosophers have already
explained. Matter cannot travel through space/time to be
in the same place at the same moment but what matters?
Where is it? If $E = MC^2$, is the opposite true?
Can this relationship be reversed?
Yes, mathematically, and no, philosophically?

Are you in the equation? Caught in the ethernet? A tourist
in cyberspace? Are you a cyborg? Who is that on the inside of the VDT
backlit like a stage set? A reflection of ourselves
or created in our image? Like a file from the computer
escape through that super-cooled liquid, the glass of the monitor's screen.
Undelete yourself. Make this mechanism scroll forward again
with its boolean logic, 0 = off, 1 = on. What does 2 do to the machine?
Does 3 equal chaos? The elegance of the discs, hard, floppy,

like hats, French cha*peaux*. The explicit sizes, 5 1/4", 3 1/2",
wondrous math symbols containing "and." Yes, navel gazing.

Or am I out of the formula? What keys to use, what keystrokes?
Writing, unable to speak, unable to think fast in company.
Drained, not stimulated by the presence of others at 12:11 a.m.
or is it p.m.? Can you tell time at noon or midnight? Can you tell right
from wrong on the spur of the moment in this continuum?
Could the "little death" become the great death? *Petit mal* become *grand mal*?
Lesions grow the way adhesions grow, or like cancer?
We don't have far to go to be part of the solution.
We are nearly all liquid.

" . . . ass Avenue"

In Grand Rapids under the sign
of a street accidentally
named for a donkey,
" . . . ass Avenue,"
the seed of youth breaks its promise,
tends to chaos instead of fruition,
like the broken husbandry
of our parent planet-
the ozone gap
over Antarctica's puce sky.

The florescent taste of tart apple
red going to blue on our adolescent
tongues, we watch a game of flies
and grounders in the home park
under our own warning yellow-green
sunset on Sunnyside Street
in a telephone spring. Long distance.

You phone from the Paris McDonald's-
Is it a *"Royale avec Cheese"*
or *"le Big Mac"* in your hand?
"Bring me 'l'eau trop chere,'
(parfum, expensive water)
dark amber," I coo into the instrument,
double-tongued, a pigeon in a birch,
like a violin double-stopped.

Fall

I hear her muffled cries
from inside your closed bedroom
as I am stuffed into a jacket
and you hoist me to your shoulders.
I ride past half sparkled windows
toward the back door where
you fly me down to slip my
feet into mom's furry boots
for taking the dog or the trash out
or bringing logs in to the stove.
My feet slide in, then out of her boots.
Your hands bruise my armpits as I rise
back up toward your shoulders.

You open the door anyway
and bump down the steps
with your hands covering my bare feet.
I hold your head, my hands in your hair,
your beer and cigarette breath steaming
the dark. We stalk the rutted lane
toward the mail and newspaper
through one of those slow snows,
huge flakes mixed with glitter.

As I look up to search for stars
you are saying something about the last
time and seeing me sometime soon,
and this is not rain inspired
by wind and snowflakes in my eyes.

Spanish Market

Santa Fé, 1995

Our parents have carefully not
taught us of our mother's heritage
to keep our minds acceptably white
in a northern city where it is better
not to be "Indian." But there
were references to her family
living in a tent, not even a teepee,
or a lodge. Forty years after
their divorce my father would still say,
"She had nothing when I married her."
His brother still speaks of her beauty.

There are deserts in America.
I hear a sun-glassed person
behind me on the Shuttle-Jack
from Albuquerque to Santa Fe and
I think of that over-rated institution,
the American family, as I return once more,
wishing for refreshment, through degrees
of heat which break a hundred-year-old record.

Along the wavering highway, not just
the effect of my bifocals, a terrapin
crosses on a path I cannot sense,
cars and pick-up trucks lurk, vapor-locked.
Jerky on the hoof, dehydrated cattle converse
on these hillsides with sage, piñon,
scrub oak. River beds salute the sun
with brilliant, dry, white gravel.
Do I hear the voice of the coyote
in this day? The keer of the hawk?

The spirit of my great-grandmother whispers
in my ear, *"Otter, tell me how*
we distinguish the air-borne hawk from
the buzzard." *"The buzzard is black beneath,*
the hawk is light," I say softly, trying to think what
depends on the yellow cactus blossom? The honeybee
or a hungry hummingbird braving the possibility
of impailment? They use so little water they
will be here longer than we.
Surely the rattlesnake does not sink fangs
here nor the scorpion arch his tail to wilt
this golden life, flashing caution.

The bus arrives in the adobe town of doors
and windows painted blue to keep out
evil spirits. There are bars on the bright
trimmed windows. In the square in front
of the Governor's Palace, Spanish Market,
retablos, santos, santeros, my cousins. The young
generation's displays of paintings inspired
by the spirituality of television violence,
the Day of the Dead, crucified skeletons,
dove of the resurrection, blood of the lamb,
furniture in sturdy Spanish style like that made
by my father, his uncle, and cousin, still used
in the inn at the end of the trail. As I walk through
the lobby beneath the music of guitars
I hear the voices, the whispered prayers
of the school of my childhood with the orphan girls
in the Mary Chapel behind the Cathedral of St. Francis.
"Children deserted," the file said after our German
nanny donated us to Catholic Social Services,
our brothers sent to Albuquerque.

Our hands bitten by the frost of the altitude,
we scratched our letters in the dead sandstone
of the playground, the difficulty of "k" or "s"
connected to "z," a challenge to the hand
and the unaccustomed tongue as I was instructed
in the language of my heritage by other children.
Mouths washed out with lye soap made by the sisters
for repeating grown-up words we didn't know
were blasphemous, girls somersaulted up the leaf-
and straw-strewn center aisle of a harvest festival.
Unable to do the tricks of the other girls,
I cried and hid my face in a nun's lap
for my near-sighted inabilities and fear
that mother would not return.
My little sister refused to go with her
when she came back. Today people seem surprised
that we are siblings, she with her black hair,
black eyes, my brown hair, hazel eyes,
but there are Natives here who look like me
and my daughter looks like her.
I have unfinished business here.

"Breathe through your nose

or this will make you cry,"
mother says as she tends
a steaming pot with her long
wooden spoon, but I am sure
I have peeled onions without a tear
or even a drop of blood
from this oak-handled knife,
too large for my hand and this chore.

Inherited from my grandmother's house,
it is the same utensil I had
my hands on under the tepid dishwater
that night my stepfather returned
from deer hunting *"Freezing,"* he said,
beer and cigarettes on his breath
as his cold canvas coat pressed
the back of my shirt. My chest
constricted, lungs hastened toward an attack
of asthma. He reached around me
and slipped his left hand under
my sweatshirt, his right down the front
of my jeans. I thought of how he slept
with a pistol on the dresser
next to the head of his bed, my mother
beside him by the alarm clock,
an orphaned moment before
we heard the door,
then his hands pulled out
of my clothes, I expelled a breath,
shuddered, and mom came back
from the neighbors.' The knife
came clean from the dishwater,
I rinsed it, placed it in the rack
to drain with more innocent flatware.

Ballet

I recall my blonde brother dancing
rock to rock in this river
flicking water-beaded nylon thread
over a surface laced with dragon flies
in a ballet we learned from our father,
my brother's heart in the water-dance,
mine in netting my catch.

I wade to the stony pool below
the shadow shelter of the trout.
A deer-fly dashes against my neck
and I have time to remember
my brother's desire for dance,
my loss; his suicide:
his response, perhaps to mockery,
and the two-step performed
with other men's wives.

I twist, fling up my arm
and the feathered hook flies
through the air, lands upstream,
floats down to that deep blue basin
twice till trout takes bait
and we are tied together.

I give the fish all the shining line
it needs, stumbling down river after it
head under water, head up,
rod held aloft through the white
rushing deep to a shallow hold for my feet.

I take a stand here, in Montana,
to reel in that lost beauty,
that flash of rainbow.

Angle of Reflection

Outside my car, in a sky clear like a blue-black bowl,
the brightest sliver moon shines through
the passenger corner of my windshield.
Why does our singular moon have a generic name,
like "man" for human, not reflecting the multiple
brands of race or gender on this planet,
unlike the multiple moons of Jupiter?

As I turn my face to look out my driver's-side window and up,
I see a fuzzy anomaly which I think is Hyakutake,
described by astronomers surprised to see it while searching
the heavens for Eros. They sight not the Greek god of love
but an asteroid of unstable orbit, a comet ten miles in diameter,
a dirty spaceball which science surmises would make a crater
the size of New York state, if it hit our Earth, would make a cloud
of debris, a shaded world, and stunt all earthly growth for years.

I turn down a county road toward my favorite pond,
low road, high water, sliver moon and Hyakutake reflected
among reeds and drowned trees in the bottom of this bowl,
to see if I can spot the first frog-fishing heron of spring.
Instead I see mud hens like dark brown bobbers
treading water nearly up to the center of the road
and beyond them, lapped by the pond, the glow of a possum
anticipating resurrection.

Maintenance

If this were his office he would have said
he had a great view of Grand Rapids, but
it is a hospital room with a hazy eye on the city.
It does not smell of naugahyde, carpeting, and
copiers, but of rubber sheets and that odor
of the bottle of vitamins in my kitchen cupboard.
I have become my father's dream of a daughter he might
have in the far future. He confuses me,
asks what I am doing here.

The cancer in his brain has returned him
to the drugged invalidism of his youth at St. Mary's.
Regressed to a time before the births of his five children,
he does not know me. Doesn't call me "Miss Muffett,"
but because I call him "Dad" and he is polite in these dreams,
he says it's nice to have children, then he wants to know
what "street drugs" I'm hiding in his food and orders
me to help him with the urinal. I tell him this is not L.A.,
and lift his gown. A nurse comes in to sample his blood
she requests with a Spanish accent. Dad mocks her
with his west coast Mexican, telling her to get some of "*that
good imported toilet paper out of the john.*" I rush
to say I will, wondering at the disappearance of his veneer
of manners, Lutheran childhood. He asks, "*What happened to me?*"
I offer him a piece of truth, "*You have pneumonia.*"

He concentrates on individual breaths,
each apnea a near release
and then he breathes again.

Angle of Repose

position of a rock on the
side of a hill or mountain incline

On a mountainside a glacier-deposited
rock rests from its travels in the embrace
of snow and ice on a tour of the continent

the way my father traveled through
his life from Michigan to Santa Fe to L.A.
seeking a warmer climate than my mother's
heart held for him. He didn't find it here
but maybe in the sunlit spot in the meadow
where a granite marker begins and ends
its history of his life. In one of those
well manicured lawns with flat stones
engraved with the Dutch names of west
Michigan and various dates in this century
and the last, ten feet from his parents,
making me think where I will lay my head
years from now, or tomorrow. He would not
discuss his immanent atheist death (the doctor
prescribed a twenty percent survival rate
and Dad demanded treatment) but negotiated
for no respiratory machinery to hum and beep
its accompaniment to the softly playing radio
the nurse brought for him to hear in those hours
while he slept his way out of the pain of his body
and its spent relationships with God.

Psych 101

Ugly dogs bark
for all the world
as if they were
good-looking.

Shooting into the Light

Lyn Coffin

Do you want to hear
the sound of one hand clapping?
Listen to your heart.

Photo by Bruce Michael Miller

*I love to muck around
in the loam of language.*

Bernini's St. Theresa

Religion's got zip to do with what's going
On here. Her swirling skirts shock you into love.
Blind as zero, you focus on her face: you're
Every inch an angel now, connoisseur of
Rosy thrills, fired by the force of knowing
The arrow you hold in your fingers will
Rivet her staggering heart. She, eyes closed, still
Orchestrates legs even Christ can't ignore:
So, angels or not, certain men from Rome,
Succinct as always, thrust God's message home.

Sometimes starting out with one of the two "edges" of a poem fixed makes me feel more confident. To write acrostics, such as the poem above, I begin by writing a friend's name down the left margin. For a sestina, I choose six favorite words and let these words "dictate" the poem cf. *Mother's Note Home*, on page 143, which consists of six six-line stanzas, with the six end-words repeated in this order: 1(*she*), 2(*dark*), 3(*light*), 4(*know*), 5(*describe*), 6(*embraces*); 6,1,2,5,3,4/ 4,6,3,1,5,2/ 2,4,5,6,1,3/ 3,2,1,4,6,5/ 5,3,6,2,4,1— followed by a tercet that contains all six .

Photo by Daryl Bright Andrews

Lyn Coffin

The Music Box

In memory of Susan Sims Coffin

There was once a magic music box. You didn't have to wind it or open its lid. If you so much as looked at it, or in its direction, it would begin to play. The song was short and rather simple, but mysterious too, because it had never been written down, and never could be. And the song you heard was different from the song your friends or neighbors heard, even if they were standing next to you in the same room, listening. Because the box was so magical, so clearly beautiful, it seemed destined to last forever. And then one day, the box began to disintegrate. The sandalwood went first, crumbling to a powder, an ash, a fine gray nothing. Then the brasswork started to lose its distinction—the pieces curled back and lost each other in themselves, in the kind of melting that is cool to the touch. Finally, the box was gone—only the mechanism remained. And everyone marveled because, still, if you so much as looked at it, or in its direction, it would start to play. The song was short and rather simple, but mysterious too, because it had never been written down, and never would be, and the song you heard was different from the song your children or parents heard, even if they were standing next to you in the same room, listening. And then one day, the mechanism itself slowly disappeared, crumbling to a powder, an ash, a fine gray nothing. And it was really only then—tomorrow, yesterday, today— that the true gift was finally revealed. For anyone having known that music had only to look where the box had been or remember it in her heart of hearts, and she heard the melody again, more clearly than before . . . Brothers and sisters, listen and say if this is not so . . . The song we hear is short and rather simple, but mysterious too, because it has never been written down, and never will be. We are listening now and forever, and the song we hear is the same.

Mother's Note Home: A Self-Portrait

Of all the dog-eared scrapbook's mysteries, she
draws my attention— standing lovely, dark
and young next to a stranger. Something— the light
or the man— frays her poise. She must know
my father— her one *note home* seems to describe
him— but he is not the man who embraces

her here. My mother never liked frank embraces
such as this— It must have offended her— She
who was so private even I can't describe
her with conviction. She held true to the dark
slide of her own life, and most of what I know,
I know through remembrances which came to light

only after her death. She could play "The Flight
of the Bumblebee"— never wore braces. She
had a pony she rode side-saddle. No
one in sixth grade had better penmanship. She
discovered art in high school, and wrote dark
poems with no misspellings trying to describe

love. In college, she stopped trying to describe
anything, rewrote "Sleeping Beauty," made light
of love. Her prince was totally in the dark—
when he kissed Beauty, he tasted the traces
of poison on her lips, and they both died . . . She
left college in her senior year for no

good reason. For years, then, there was nothing— no
notes or pictures except the one to describe
what must have happened. But with my birth, she
returned— On a stiff white card, she drew a light
bulb, my name and weight, and picked up the traces
of her life. There follows a series of dark

snapshots: infant, toddler, Girl Scout (I'm the dark
one on the end). High School. College. Grad school. No
heart-tugs in these, just seas of frozen faces,
till the last. I see me starting to inscribe
a book of poems under a bookstore spotlight.
My mother's not in these pictures because she

took them. But my poems explore longings she lived
and she taught me the one principle I know:
Whatever light describes, the dark embraces.

Chant for Nicole

Lyn Coffin

I stare at her, she stares at me, sister to sister, both of us blind.
     oh, say you can see
Blood on the Bronco, reddish brown flecks on the driver's door,
a spray of spots on the passenger side, a speck or two
on the instrument panel, blots on the mat on the driver's side, drops
on the rubber on the driver's floor, spatters on the seat and
the steering wheel, streaks on the console, a blotch on the backrest,
a splash on the curb, a splatter on the drive, a skein on the wall
of the open garage, splotches on the walk, stains in the foyer,
Blood in the bathroom, Blood in the bedroom,
Blood on the paws of a barking dog,
I'm beyond belief with Bleeding and Blood,
I can't see beyond the surf and the surfeit,
beyond beyond I'm wearing her Blood—
Blood like a badge, a burden, like nothing but Blood—
Blood like a tide, a flood, a decision,
Blood on the Bible, blood in the stool,
Blood like a telegram under the door,
Blood drying sticky on tissues and towels,
Blood on the tiles, on the bricks, on the ivy,
Blood like a woman making dinner alone,
Blood like a flag, Blood like a bank vault,
Blood like an engine, Blood like a sermon, a chair in the corner,
Blood like a well, like a signed requisition,
Blood like a girl with long legs and long fingers,
Blood like a man with a gun to his head,
Blood like a bubble, Blood like a bargain,
Blood like a seed, Blood like belief, like goodbye, like a wishbone,
Blood like a dark ship rocking at anchor,
Blood like a warning, Blood like a dog in a hurry for home,
Blood like a ticket, Blood like a phone call,
Blood like a number, a premise, a preview, a silence, a soap box,
a marriage, a mix-up, an opera, an outcry, a business, a *custom* . . .
east and west goes her rigorous mouth—
her throat keeps grinning from north to south—
down in the valley all of us stare—
bound in red rivers of bright yellow hair.

Crystals of the Unforeseen

In the thinning night, the stars draw closer—
children around a sickroom, whispering.
Nobody ever knows what will happen . . .
Even the window's being opened by
a gust of wind was unexpected— Death
we wait for, but he lands disguised— some
Odysseus, some minor injury—
delicate as a change in coloration,
a knot hidden like a tiny island
under the untroubled sea of our skin
a ragged tremolo in our breathing.
Every cut or band-aid, every bone we
gnaw clean during normal dinner is
a blue rubber band around our wrist—
We're careful to stop on our way home,
but can't remember whether to get milk
or dog food. No matter how we watch for him
Death just comes— We hear a thump on our porch
one night, and in the morning, there he is
like a free subscription— or a messenger
from the king, with one glass slipper we
need to try. And what are birds who slam into
our bayside windows? What are phone calls
in the cutthroat hours, or the miniature
explosions which mark the end of light bulbs,
what are even the children we actually
wanted if not crystals of the unforeseen?
So when love, that impecunious stranger
comes banging at our back door on his way
to every back door in the neighborhood,
selling whatever it is he's selling,
looking for whoever's home with a checkbook,
we're ready to spend, more than willing
to buy the latest in magazines or
blenders, hot to give any God a chance.

Shooting into the Light

Adam motioned to John to come closer. "I thought we'd skirt along the south edge of Lost Lake," he said. John just nodded and looked away. Adam had warned himself about that, told himself not to expect too much of the kid the first time out.

John was just scared— scared of letting his father down. Adam had been the same way, all those years ago. Of course, he'd been younger. Some people might have said there was a world of difference between ten and eighteen, but Adam knew better. The first time hunting was the first time hunting. Hell, he'd been thirty when he married Doris, and all his years of messing around hadn't made one amen of difference. The first time was always the first time.

He looked down at the 10 gauge in his arms, then over at John's 30.06 Mossberg, then back. He hefted the shotgun. His grandfather had the stock made from mahogany, and carved it himself. The guys called it the biggest gun in the world. Three generations of Michigan Carbecks had carried her on shoots. John would have been the fourth, but John wouldn't carry her. He told his mom he'd go this once, but he wasn't going to use a shotgun. Shotguns were for butchers, he said. A lot he knew.

The sun was pasted up high in the east, pale and flat like Doris's throat discs. Other hunters had staked out bar space hours ago, but "let the boy sleep," Doris kept saying. Never mind. It was better this way, even if the sun was hot and made you dizzy, like drinking before lunch. It was good just the two of them out here. Or could be.

He looked at John. The kid could never get hold of an expression for his face. Times like now, he looked one way one minute and another the next. Maybe he wanted to talk about his mother's dying. Her condition, he called it. Or maybe he wanted to say why, after years of telling Adam *no*, he'd let Doris talk him into it. Probably not, though. John was never much for talking.

"This is as good a place as any to separate," Adam said when they got to the jack pine at the edge of the grove. He said it casually, but John looked as if he might jump right out of his skin. "I thought the whole point of this thing was for us to do it together," he said.

Adam couldn't figure it. Doris had been dying for weeks and John had handled it okay. Now, all of a sudden, he was riled up. Adam remembered something Doris had said last night in the sticky voice the pills gave her. "Your ma says you got girl trouble," he said aloud. "Is that right?" The kid flushed up, cursed under his breath, and said in a voice that diced the words, "Never mind that. Where do you want me to go?"

Adam nodded. The kid knew these woods like the back of his hand, and had been a top marksman in school, but none of that mattered now. Now was different. Now was the real article. Adam made his voice as soft as he could. "Just stay put, and get yourself ready. I'll circle behind Barber's old field and see if I can't scare something down to you. You're a fool not to use a clip, though, scope or no scope." Adam could tell the kid was mad by the way he dug in the toe of his sneaker, but he wouldn't look at Adam. Nobody looked at anything straight on these days unless it was the goddamned t.v. "I've got another bullet in my pocket," John said, as though that settled everything.

The path between the lumber cut and Barnaby's Ridge led through a trough of poison sumac. The bushes looked cheerful in the high sun, and they were all pretty much chest height. Walking through them was like pushing through a playground of kids, but it was the shortest way to get where he was going. Adam criss-crossed down the hill and came out in back of where Barber's sugar beets had been. Everyone had told Sam Barber you couldn't grow beets on ridgeland, but he wouldn't listen. His farm went belly up and everybody felt sorry for him until he went away and made a fortune in underwear. Just one more in a long line of things that went to show you couldn't tell.

He stayed close to the pine, using the thick carpet of needles to cushion his steps. An old Indian trick. Most of the tricks were. He thought at first there was nothing in the field, and he told himself that was okay. There were a lot of other places to try, and he'd try all of them. If the boy didn't have a good day, he wouldn't be back. That was how he was. Even with all the places, the chances of having a good day the first time out were less than nothing. Adam started looking out of the corners of his eyes. The thing about hunting was seeing like a deer, like you had eyes on the sides of your head.

The buck was standing way over to the south side of the field, about fifty yards away, but a clear shot. Adam sighted, feeling the old thrill as the buck's image sharpened into certainty. Then he re-cradled the gun. He could probably get him, even with the 10 gauge, though it was meant for close work. But having heard his father shoot a deer wouldn't mean anything to the boy. He was that much a Carbeck at any rate.

Adam kept circling, keeping to the edge of the field, where the grass was thick and the soil was still, after all these years, broken up and crumbly. He didn't make a sound that he could hear.

He'd planned to get up on the far side of the buck and send him bounding toward the kid with a scare-shot, like they did in those late-night movies Doris liked, but he didn't have time. The buck got wind of him right away and took off on a fast, jagged trot, like a Ford with no shocks. Adam thought of firing anyway, to warn the kid. Let him think the buck had gotten away from his father and John'd probably try all the harder. But that was another thing that went against the Carbeck grain, doing anything needlessly. So Adam cradled the gun a little tighter, and waited.

From where he stood, the shot sounded like nothing more than a New Year's noisemaker, but it made Adam jump a little anyway. He must have been more nervous than he thought. He waited a minute more and there was nothing. The forest had been quiet before, but now it was silent.

Adam headed back. He knew better than to run but kept on at a steady pace, floundering sometimes in patches of soft gray sand that collected like water between ridges. It bothered him there wasn't a second shot. Most likely the kid had missed.

He rounded the bend, jogging now down the middle of the dry creek bed the way the buck had come, and there was John, the deer lying on the ground not five feet in front of him. Adam walked over to his son in silence. He wanted to pound the miracle of his luck into him. "Do you know how many shots it took me?" he wanted to say. "A lot. That's how many." But he'd do better to let John have the first word. Best not to come barreling up and say something he'd regret later. The boy's face had a blue-white shadow to it now, like the powdered milk stuff the doctor had ordered for Doris when he thought it was just her stomach. Adam felt funny looking at the kid, so he looked at the deer. The boy had done his grandfather proud. Maybe those riflery classes had gotten through to him after all. A nice clean hole right where a line from the ear and a line from the eye would have crossed. There wasn't any mess Adam could see. The kid must've hit him from a good three hundred yards. The buck was a small six-pointer, not more than 100 pounds, which meant only 60, dressed. Still . . .

The kid made a gargling sound. Adam looked up. John was glaring at him, eyes so wide they seemed to straddle his face like glasses. He took a step back from Adam, from the buck, and stretched out his hands, the rifle balanced across them. Adam thought at first the boy was handing him the gun. Maybe he didn't know the buck had had it, and he wanted Adam to finish up. Adam reached out but John took a step backward, dropped the rifle on the ground and stood there, weaving back and forth. "That's it, Dad," John said. "That's as far as I go, even for her." He passed his hand over his eyes and when he looked at Adam again it was like he couldn't see. He turned and walked heavily off at a drunken slant, as though his feet were the last things to move. "Come on, Johnny," Adam said. "You can't just walk off and leave me here."

But that was exactly what the boy did. Adam watched until he was out of sight. The blond hair bounced against the red and black squares of the jacket. He could walk away and leave his father to clean up after him. He could come home last Christmas and act all choked up and go right back to school when vacation was over, leaving Adam instead of a nurse to rub the bed sores out of his mother— because there was only so much money and John came first, John and his college education. Adam had a crazy impulse to aim the biggest gun in the world right into the middle of all that brightness.

The thing was how to get the deer home. He picked up the kid's rifle and tossed it where the wild grape and ivy were thickest. He would make the kid come back for it later. But that was like something the kid would do. He walked over and retrieved it, plunging his bare hand up to the wrist in dusty green leaves and berries the color of old blood.

He tucked the 10-gauge high up under his left arm, the rifle under his right, so both hands were free. Grabbing a hind leg in each hand, he began a back-pull. He had pulled John out of the bathroom like this— broken down the door and dragged him out, Doris holding up the kid's head when it came to going down the stairs and out to the car. So many ups and downs, so many doors. The doctors told Doris it had been a near thing. Take the kid to a shrink, they'd said. For months, all Doris talked about was suicidal tendencies and the kid kept talking about what had made him try to off himself until Adam wanted to scream— *did* scream late one night, told them both to shut up and let him eat the stinking casserole.

It was hotter than he'd realized. The sun was everywhere, which was part of why you were supposed to go in the morning or evening. Try as he would to settle his hat, branches kept knocking it off.

The deer was heavier than John had been, heavier even than Doris, that time she'd fainted in the bar and he'd dragged her into bed and called the doctor and the doctor said over the phone there was nothing to worry about.

The guns kept trying to slide. His arms and sides ached from the effort of holding them. He thought of taking them out to the truck and coming back for the deer. But somebody'd steal them out of the truck as fast as he turned his back. The kid had locked the keys inside once, and Adam'd had to pry the door open. Since then, the driver's lock didn't work.

It was too hot for a Michigan fall. Adam stopped. He put the rifle under his right arm, the 10-gauge under his left. That felt better at first, but after a minute, he changed them back. He could feel sweat beading under his wool collar and oozing down his back. There was a belt of sweat around his waist.

The buck was a dead weight, that was the problem. Maybe he could take it out to the road first, then come back for the guns. No. Some weekender would jump at the chance to claim a nice buck as his own. A quick switch of the deer from one pickup to another and, bingo, instant hero, a rich man's meat on the table for weeks. If Doris could keep it down, it might even do the trick there. She had a taste for deer meat, she said.

The buck's antlers dragged in the gray sand, and his front feet moved in the leaves sometimes as if half of him were still alive. His hind legs kept slipping out of Adam's hands. Adam tightened his grip. He'd like to strangle the kid sometimes. To hell with the kid, anyway. To hell with all kids.

When he got to the shoulder of Old 23, there was no sign of the truck. He thought for a second he'd gotten the wrong logging trail and come out of the woods somewhere else. It was hotter yet out of the trees. The asphalt road cooked in the sun. Flies started buzzing around his eyes, mosquitoes whined in his ears. But, no, it was the right trail. Had to be. And then he realized. He'd let the kid drive just to show he didn't hold the busted door against him and of course he hadn't thought to get the keys back. So the kid, who was used to hitching, had turned around and helped himself to the truck and was probably having a good laugh to himself along about now, thinking what a joke it was to take his father's truck and leave him the buck and rifles to deal with.

Adam pulled the buck up onto the shoulder of the road and squatted beside it, both guns still under his arms. Two cars went by without slowing down, so he tried standing. It didn't make any difference. If anything, they went by faster— three, four, seven. The deer's dusty red tongue lolled up at him in a big dead grin. Ha Ha. It was too hot for fall. The kid'd left him high and dry. He was sweating like a pig. Goddamn the kid anyway.

A pickup came barreling around the corner from town, and he thought for a minute the kid had changed his mind. The driver even looked like John. Adam waved, but the kid-driver only whizzed on by.

Finally, a Chevy came down the road. It was pretty old by the sound of it. Adam stepped out on the road and turned to face that way. The car kept coming and coming. *Come on ahead*, Adam thought. *Run me down*. But then at the last second his nerve failed him and he jumped aside, off the road. He didn't think it was going to stop, but it did— pulled up right next to him in a cloud of dust that made tears crowd into his eyes. A big-shouldered girl in overalls with a blobby face and no hair to speak of was driving. There were three other teenagers— boys or girls, who could tell?— in the back and a boy with long dark hair that hung down over his face like a dog's was sitting up in front with the girl. He had his left hand resting on the girl's leg, way above the knee. It was a big hand, a man's hand. It didn't seem to belong to the face.

"What's the trouble, Dad?" asked Dog Boy with a know-it-all

smile. The rear-view mirror was cockeyed. Adam saw him wink at the kids in the back. "Cut your hair," Adam wanted to say. "Get a job. Don't call me Dad. Sit up. Get your hand off her leg."

"I said, "What can we do for you, Dad?" Dog Boy said. His chin was dotted red with pimples and yellowed over with some kind of powder.

Adam took off his hat and resettled it, feeling how the ring of cold sweat circled his head. He was doing the right thing, he told himself. He had to see it through, for everyone's sake.

"Ooh, look at the deer!" the girl said suddenly, as if she was just now seeing it. Laughter came from the back seat. Dog Boy leaned way out the window, his face coming straight for Adam's gut as if he was going to kiss him there. He turned his head at the last second. His lips were wet and pink like he'd put on lipstick and hadn't wiped it all off. Adam shook himself. Dog Boy pulled his head back in. "You want a lift?"

"I'd appreciate it," Adam said. And was sorry.

Dog Boy winked in the mirror again. "You just climb right in and we'll take you where you're going," he said. "But I'm afraid your girl friend'll have to wait— unless you want to ride with her in your lap."

It took Adam a minute to realize Dog Boy meant the deer. He couldn't leave the deer. "That's okay," Adam told him. "I'll just—"

"Wait a sec," Dog Boy said. "Why don't I just find some rope and we'll tie her on top?" He didn't move.

"That's okay," Adam said. "I—"

"No, really, Dad. I think a good strong rope is the solution to the whole problem, you know what I mean?" Dog Boy's hand was walking up and down the girl's leg like a big white spider. Adam must have nodded because the kid reached out ever so slowly, opened the glove box, and took out a piece of clothesline, which he dangled in the window. It was about as long as a garden snake. "Mercy, Dad," Dog-Boy said. "Looks like we've come up a mite short, don't it?" He began— all of them began— a laugh they never finished. It stopped and Dog Boy raised his hands. "Take it easy now, Dad."

It was so good to have Dog Boy's hands up in the air, away from the girl's privates, it took Adam a second to realize he'd let the rifle slide and tilt until the barrel came to rest in the crook of his arm, not exactly pointing at anything, not exactly not. He must have stepped back because Dog Boy's face seemed far away. "Get out and help me, you hear?" Adam said, and he was surprised because it seemed exactly the thing to say.

"Sure enough, Dad," Dog Boy said. "Just let me make myself presentable." He held up the piece of clothesline again, took an end in each hand, slowly put it over his head, back and under all the straggly hair. Suddenl,y Adam saw what Dog Boy was doing. He was tying back his hair, tying it into a pony tail. In a moment, he would wink in the mirror again.

Adam stepped back and straightened. Somebody in the car said something about shooting into the light, and there was a noiseless flash that made his eyes spin, and the world went black and red, black and red, like somebody's checkerboard jacket, and all at once he was at a dance called a "square dance" where people went around in circles, and his daddy laughed and whirled faster than anyone, with the lady whose mouth made a little red "o"— the prettiest lady, except for his mother, who stood with her back to the wall, not smiling, and he rushed out in the center to stop his father, to stop them all, and found himself being whirled around by the lady with the red mouth so his feet didn't even touch the ground, and afterward his mother said he was like his father, and he said, he wasn't, he hadn't wanted to do it, he hadn't liked it at all, and she said, "Don't lie to me, boy, you thought you was in high cotton."

Dog Boy was waving a camera in front of Adam's face. Keeping the 10 gauge pressed against his right side, Adam raised the rifle barrel. He pulled the trigger and waited for death to happen. But there was only a click and Dog Boy said "Let's stop kidding around, okay, Dad?" And Dog Boy was smiling his same smile, he was winking that same wink again, winking right at the rifle, his blue eyes and milky face was all there was, and it didn't matter how many triggers Adam pulled, they were nothing in the face of the Dog Boy face, the face of the way things were, that filled up the world like the broadside of a barn that couldn't be hit, because the closer you got, the bigger it was. So the bullet earmarked for Dog Boy's brain was in the kid's pocket, and the bullet and the pocket and the kid and the truck were gone. And if he aimed the 10 gauge and blasted

Whoever straight down the path to Kingdom Come, so what? They were all going that road anyway, so what was the goddamn hurry?

Dog Boy started talking again, but now Adam had better sense than to listen. He walked around the front of the car, eyes fixed on the girl at the wheel. The woman driver. The key. He stood by her door, steadying himself on the running board with the shotgun butt. Her window was down, as if she'd been expecting him.

"What's your name, honey?" The first words he'd said to Doris.

There were hoots from the back. The girl reddened. "Sammy," she said. Then, "Samantha."

More hoots.

"Is this your car, Samantha?"

"So what if it is?"

"Nothing, Samantha. Only I'd be grateful if you'd ditch your friends here as soon as you decently can and come back for me and the deer." Adam took off his hat and shielded his eyes. He willed the girl to look at him, to really look, and just for a second she did. He leaned toward her, his mouth where the window would have been. He was almost whispering in her ear. "I'll make it worth your while, Samantha," he said. "I promise."

The car leapt forward. He heard the girl's voice— "Shut up, you guys!" Hard to believe it was the same voice that had said, "Samantha."

He found the rifle and laid the shotgun crosswise on it. "X marks the spot," he said aloud. Then he walked over to the deer. Samantha would come back. Or John. Or somebody he'd never met would stop and pick him up, deer and all. He sat in the dust, pushing the deer's legs apart and easing himself back until he could feel the belly warm and solid against his spine. He stretched his legs. He and the buck were a six-legged beast from a kid story.

Legs is the word for the day, he told himself. Behind him, the deer's belly responded, moving in and out with every breath he took . . . Doris had been so pretty.

He wasn't mad or sad or anything at all. Just curious to see what would happen next. He closed his eyes and settled down to wait. What else was there to do?

Point of View Problems

Jack was fifty-six, Carolyn was fifty-one. Between them, they had six ex-spouses, six grown children, and one hundred and seven years of experience. They both listed themselves as writers. According to the dating service, they were perfect for each other.

Jack gave Carolyn one of his stories to read at the conclusion of their first date.

On their second date, Jack asked Carolyn what she thought of the story. She said it had point of view problems. She didn't like the way the story shifted back and forth from the male protagonist's to the female protagonist's point of view, she said.

Jack thought by Carolyn's reactions that she was probably somewhat of a prude. He had hoped Carolyn would see beneath the sexual skin of the story the poignancy of Jackson's plight, his struggle to escape his mother.

Then Jack decided he had been unfair to Carolyn. He had more or less been expecting the two of them to fall into mental bed together, but Carolyn was a bright woman, he reminded himself. Bright women, for whom he'd asked the dating service— bright women didn't just fall into bed, mental or otherwise, with you. That was part of what made them bright. You had to talk about yourself first, let them get to know you. And not just the pretty stuff, either, or they'd think you were conning them. Jack decided to give Carolyn the benefit of a considerable doubt and, for most of the second date, talked about his troubled past. Jack had had a lot of physical and emotional pain following operations on an inguinal hernia, operations which caused iatrogenic problems.

Jack liked the way Carolyn was able to keep up with him. She skipped right over words like "inguinal" and "iatrogenic" like a flat stone over waves. On the down side of things, there did seem to be large gaps in her knowledge. He saw her as Chaucer's gap-toothed prioress— that led to an image of his having at her from behind, which led him to a memory of his last girl friend who gave him a wrought-iron lawn ornament which he'd first mistaken for a mushroom but which turned out to be a woman bending over. Carolyn thought Jack's pains sounded insignificant compared to her recent mastectomy. But Kendall, her third ex, had been virtually monosyllabic for the last six years of their marriage, so she found Jack's torrent of words like a waterfall— initially refreshing, if ultimately numbing. She liked the way Jack zipped from topic to topic and she got to dart in and out of the weave of his monologue.

Carolyn gave Jack one of her stories on their second date. Jack found the story more than a little disquieting. One of the suspects— "a real thug with dark, bushy eyebrows and squinty eyes"— looked more than a little like him, just for starters. It seemed ominous Carolyn's first fictional communiqué was about death and craziness and a marriage in which the husband saw his wife as "a boulder he was trying to roll uphill, away from the tomb."

Jack was not reassured when, during their third date, Carolyn gave him a run-down of what she called her past lives and referred offhandedly to a number of suicide attempts, at one point waving her wrists in front of his nose so he could see the scars.

Carolyn was disappointed in Jack's reaction to her stories, fictional and otherwise. She had hoped Jack would feel reassured that she was different from the unbalanced, sex-starved women in his past. She had converted late to sanity and, like most converts, was especially secure in her faith.

On their next date, he brought her an article he'd written for the Psychodynamic Quarterly, on "The Blood-Dimmed Tide: Lawrence and the Mind/Body Duality."

"It was Yeats who wrote about blood-dimmed tides," Carolyn said.

"I know that very well," Jack told her.

"I like the way you say *very*," she said, stirring the coke she had told him made it impossible for her to sleep at night. "You make it rhyme with *furry*."

"One has to be intellectually honest if he writes," he told her.

"Your problem," she said, making the phrase include more than literature, "is excessive use of the passive voice— that's from your being a scholar." She spat the last word out as though it were a term of abuse, but her correct use of the possessive case pleased Jack.

He rummaged in his briefcase and produced a pack of Marlboros. "Sorry, Jack," Carolyn said, sounding not sorry at all. "I'm going to have to ask you not to smoke."

"I thought you told the agency smoking was okay."

"I told them considerate smoking was okay."

Jack sighed and put his cigarettes in his breast pocket, where they would be more accessible. "What is considerate smoking, anyway?" he asked.

"Considerate means privately," Carolyn said. "So, you teach English?"

That was women in a nutshell, Jack decided. They had no use for segues except in business meetings— otherwise, their trains of thought kept jumping the tracks. "Actually," he told her, "I teach history of art at the prison."

"Milan?" Respect flared in Carolyn's eyes.

"No," Jack said, trying to keep his voice afloat. "Tecumseh."

The image of Jack facing mortal danger, a man among men, faded in front of Carolyn's eyes. "Tecumseh doesn't have a prison," she said.

Jack shook his head. The less women knew, the surer they were, even the bright ones. "They'd better," he said. "Otherwise I'm wasting my time there three nights a week."

"Oh, night school," Carolyn said.

"It's a woman's prison," Jack told her.

Carolyn saw a picture of Jack in a turban surrounded by large black women in leg shackles singing and carrying plates of food. *No racial stereotyping,* she admonished herself— *they're probably all anorexic lesbian accountants from Bloomfield Hills.* She was getting restless. "So that's how scholars make a living," she said.

Jack saw himself sleeping in an underground cave. Carolyn came in with a candle— She bent over him. "What do you do at night?" He tried to make it an erotic question.

"Nothing that makes me money, I can assure you," Carolyn said.

Jack felt first apologetic, then resentful —he hadn't done anything to feel apologetic about. "You told DateLiners you were a writer," he said. It came out more as an accusation than a question.

"Most men want my measurements," Carolyn said. "You want my vitae. Is that it?"

Jack patted his breast pocket, to make sure his cigarettes were still there. They were.

"What's that all about?" Carolyn wanted to know. She fought the impulse to fold her arms across her chest.

"What's what all about?"

"You expect me to believe you're genuinely bewildered?"

"I am genuinely bewildered," Jack said. "My bewilderment's the most genuine thing about me."

Carolyn's palpable dislike of him slid off her face like snow off a roof. She started to laugh. Jack started to laugh, too.

"I'm sorry," Carolyn said. "When I mentioned my measurements, you started patting your chest. I thought you were making fun of me."

"I'm just an addict in need of reassurance," Jack explained, not catching her drift. He raised the cigarette pack so she could see it, then let it drop back.

He saw himself parting her dark hair and kissing the nape of her neck.

She saw the two of them lying down in a room with scented candles.

They moved in together, had sex infrequently for six years, split up, ended in separate nursing homes. Neither of them got involved again. They both died in their sleep.

The Psychiatrist's Second Wife

The psychiatrist's second wife was tall and lanky and not at all suited to gardening. Nevertheless, she was out that March day trying to put a Kroger bagful of "Early Miracle" bulbs in the still semi-frozen rock garden between the house and his semi-detached office. Thus it was that she happened to overhear an overweight woman patient inquire about the psychiatrist's new dog, Annie. The psychiatrist explained to the patient as he walked her to her car, that his wife had let a good male friend hand over Annie to them, because she was a soft-hearted person open to that kind of thing.

What he did not tell the patient was that his wife's good male friend was her first husband. The psychiatrist did not mention that his wife had fallen in love with him, and he with her, during their therapy together, when he was her psychiatrist. He had gone home immediately, consequent to their first love-making (during her regularly scheduled hour, on the office couch) and told his first wife, with whom he now shared the custody of one adopted daughter, that he was going to file for divorce.

The daughter had been adopted following an automobile accident in a car, which had been delivered to the psychiatrist and his first wife minus shoulder straps—despite the psychiatrist's having stipulated that he wanted them. The psychiatrist had wanted to refuse the car, but his first wife was unwilling to make a fuss. The night of that same day, a drunk driver being chased by police, hit the psychiatrist's car head on and, because the psychiatrist's first wife was not wearing a shoulder strap, her seat belt had nearly cut her in two like a magician's saw, terminating a pregnancy he hadn't known about, and almost ending her life.

These were some of the many things the psychiatrist did not tell his patient, at least within earshot of his lanky second wife. The psychiatrist obviously felt what he did say about their adoption of a second dog, his wife's openness to that sort of thing, his own tolerance, was more than sufficient.

So that evening, the psychiatrist's wife (I am speaking of myself, of course; I have embedded my own character in my own story, though why this should matter to anyone, I cannot possibly fathom) received a phone call from the overweight patient, offering her, the wife, and by implication, the shadowy psychiatrist husband, the ownership of a three- year-old unneutered male Sheltie of championship lines, recently returned to the kennel of the patient's good friend (her ex-husband, perhaps?) after misplacement in an unhealthy environment.

The psychiatrist's wife's friend Aaron was over for dinner that evening, as he so often was. Aaron was twenty-five, ten years younger than she, and good-looking in a rabbinical, off-the-wall sort of way. They had been friends from the moment they met in the Kroger's produce aisle, both reaching for the same purple cabbage. The psychiatrist's wife had brought Aaron home with her straight from Kroger's, because that's the sort of person she tried to be. She and the psychiatrist had gotten married the week before, and she was more than a little apprehensive about his reaction. But the psychiatrist had made it immediately clear there was no need for concern on anyone's part, least of all his. The psychiatrist seemed to consider Aaron in the light of another of his second wife's adopted strays, insofar as he considered Aaron at all.

There had been moments— days, nights— when Aaron and the psychiatrist's second wife could easily have become lovers. The psychiatrist's second wife couldn't have told anyone why the strong erotic tension between her and Aaron had never translated itself into action. But she had a picture of their situation that she assumed he shared. She saw the two of them at the top of a long, curving slide— he in the back, she in the front, between his long legs. The kids below them yelled, but they were agreed on a course of non-action and stayed right where they were, liking the way the moment fit them. They knew it was their moment, and they made it last as long as they could.

Now, with the prospect of the Sheltie coming into focus, the psychiatrist's wife tried to get Aaron to take the animal, but he pleaded the usual excuses (restrictive lease, vacations away), and confessed he didn't have her way with animals. She openly doubted that, citing his stellar relations with her two dogs and the psychiatrist's daughter. Aaron acknowledged the truth of this but added ruefully, "Ah, yes, but that's only because they don't belong to me."

And so on a Saturday in late March, two weeks before Easter, the dog they were to name *"Shelley"* arrived. The psychiatrist, his second wife, the overweight patient, the psychiatrist's adopted daughter, and the kennel owner stood at the end of the long dirt driveway and watched as Shelley ran to and fro with his neck-chain dangling, doing his business, marking his territory with a vengeance, as the psychiatrist said, to the general boredom of the two female dogs already in residence. It was agreed there was to be a trial period of a week, after which a decision would be made, and Shelley returned to the kennel, or papers forwarded from there. This much was hammered out in intense negotiations since, as the kennel owner put it, she didn't usually provide papers with freebies. The contractual arrangements being concluded, the patient and the kennel owner took off in the kennel owner's van, leaving Shelley behind.

Almost a week went by without any relevant problems. The dog ran away once, but he was picked up by the Humane Society a day later, or at least a dog answering his description was. The psychiatrist's wife went to get the dog and pay the fees. But when the psychiatrist's wife saw the dog in the cage, he looked so beautiful and so frightened, she wasn't sure it was the same dog. He was not wearing a collar

This put her in an ethical dilemma— small, but with manifold implications. Should she confidently claim the dog, anyway? Or should she admit her uncertainty to the personnel? She chose the latter course, and explained. The result was half an hour of bureaucratic interrogation, at the end of which she claimed to have recognized the dog, after all. The staff people must have known she was lying, but they let her take the animal home without further protest or remark.

The confusion at the shelter had made the psychiatrist's wife even less sure of the dog's being the right one, and it came as a reassurance to her to see that when she and Shelley reached home, the other dogs appeared to recognize him immediately, especially the wife's collie-retriever, named *"Fa"* by her ex-husband for "fait accompli." As a matter of fact, Shelley's return from the Humane Society initiated a new phase of canine relations. Although Fa had been fixed years ago, prior to any litter of puppies, in a successful attempt to help her maintain her equable good nature, both Shelley and Fa appeared to be blissfully unaware of the scientific state of things. Shelley constantly had his nose under Fa's tail, and there was much licking, on his part, of both ends of Fa. The expression on Fa's face as Shelley licked was a mixture of boredom, wariness, and satisfaction. Annie, the poodle-mix, moved to the other end of the porch while this was going on. She lay down, closed her eyes, and then wagged her stumpy tail fitfully, as if to say anything was okay with her as long as she wasn't required to play a part.

The psychiatrist and his wife decided to adopt Shelley. To mark the decision, the psychiatrist took a Polaroid snapshot of his wife holding the dog in her lap as she sat at the breakfast table; he put it up on the refrigerator door under a pineapple magnet that said "Hawaii." The psychiatrist and his wife talked vaguely of breeding Shelley to the overweight patient's collie, Mignon, and of making supplemental income in this way. The psychiatrist was no good at making money or keeping the money he made. The problem had to do with the "sliding scale" he charged, on the one hand, and the IRS on the other. If he made enough money, the psychiatrist told his second wife, he would be willing to think about her wish to start a second family.

The day before Easter, the dog's papers came in the mail. Then came Easter afternoon. Shelley and Fa and Annie had been locked out on the back porch, where Shelley had been, as far as one could tell from the mixture of barks and growls issuing thence, bothering Fa, and one look out the kitchen door was sufficient to assure the psychiatrist's wife that Fa was requesting to be let in so she might retire to her solitary spot in the corner of the living room, under the psychiatrist's wife's baby grand piano. The psychiatrist's wife opened the kitchen door, and tried to get Fa inside while keeping Shelley out. To that end, she held his new collar with her left hand, while coaxing Fa forward with her right. What this triggered in Shelley's mind was anybody's guess. But the fact of the matter was this: without giving any sign— no ears back, no furrowed upper lip, no growl, Shelley turned his beautiful aquiline head and sank his teeth deep into the psychiatrist's wife's left hand.

Her first reaction was one of anger, an anger built on fear like a skyscraper on sand. She heard herself say "Ouch" and hated the childish cast of her voice. She stood, blood dripping, and said in a more normal, adult tone—"Jesus Christ." With her good hand, she tipped over a lightweight lawn table and kicked it in the dog's direction. The dog stood in a corner of the porch. He appeared to be attempting eye contact with Fa, who had slipped behind the psychiatrist's wife and was now pressing a wet nose into the crook of her right knee.

The psychiatrist's wife slammed back into the house. Aaron stood by the sink where he had been washing dishes, watching her entrance with what appeared to be a mixture of quizzicality and alarm. The psychiatrist's wife pushed past Aaron, leaned over the stainless steel sink, and rinsed her hand, first with warm, then with colder and colder water. Aaron put his arm around her. "It'll be all right," he said. "Everything will be all right." He did not ask what had happened. Maybe he had seen it all. It didn't matter. She didn't like getting reassurances from Aaron. She was supposed to reassure *him*.

After a minute, the psychiatrist's wife said softly, as if in her own defense— "Would you get him, please?" "Sure," Aaron said, his cheerfulness, as always, masking hurt, in a way calculated to make her feel responsible.

The psychiatrist came in the kitchen a few minutes later, Aaron tagging behind him. The psychiatrist was in the middle of redecorating his office. He was barefoot and shirtless, despite the coldness of the day. There was paint spattered on his work pants, which had lost both their pockets and were torn. There was paint on his wire-rimmed glasses, his fingers, his chin. He did not look the part to take charge of anything, but take charge he did. First, he produced a box of cotton balls from under the sink, and stopped the bleeding. Next, he asked Aaron to look after his daughter "for the duration." Then he put on sneakers and a shirt, bundled his wife up in her winter coat, and took her to the hospital.

There they waited in line for a nurse to see the psychiatrist's wife and make a determination as to whether she needed urgent or emergent care.

Finally, the psychiatrist's wife was wheeled into an examination room. She lay down on the kind of bed she associated so shamefully with yearly gynecological exams. The psychiatrist retreated to the waiting room, in search of magazines.

The doctor entered. He stood at her side, looking down at her. The room was swimming. He identified himself as Dr. Hertz, and someone laughed. The psychiatrist's wife was confused. Everything was happening somewhere else. Pain had turned her into a skipping stone.

Dr. Hertz said the hand was especially susceptible to infection because of its compartmental nature. He said therefore he would like to be aggressive in his approach. He produced a needle. But before he could "poke around" in the large, tri-cornered tear at the base of her thumb, he had to pull off the blood-soaked cotton balls. Dr. Hertz muttered something, then shook his head. "Who's responsible for this?" he asked, as if he expected an answer.

After Dr. Hertz had cleaned and disinfected "the problem area," he injected a local anesthetic. Dr. Hertz held her hand for a moment while the anesthetic took effect, then began to baste her hand with water.

Dr. Hertz explained that this would be the most beneficial and painful part of the treatment, since anesthetics only numbed sharp sensations and would do nothing to block or counteract any painful internal pressure put on tissue by irrigation water.

All came to pass as he had suggested. The pain was terrific. Finally, Dr. Hertz announced himself satisfied.

Should she wish to, Dr. Hertz said, the psychiatrist's wife could come back to him in two days, when a doctor would need to look at her wound and verify the absence of any infection. She wanted to ask him how one verified an absence. She felt this was an important point. She wanted to ask the doctor— a medical doctor, a hospital doctor, a real doctor— if she could stay there, flat on her back, having her hand held, on a bed in the middle of the urgent care unit on the ground floor of the state's largest hospital. But of course she did nothing of the kind.

She wanted to walk but the psychiatrist insisted she get in a wheelchair so she could get the free ride he was paying an arm and a leg for. He wheeled her out to the car and they drove home.

When they got home, Aaron had raked a large pile of leaves, left over from the previous fall, exposed when the last snow had finally melted. He did not look at her particularly, nor make any of his usual excuses to touch her. But he took the four of them out to dinner, paying the check with a wad of small bills, and she knew what that meant on many levels.

The psychiatrist and the psychiatrist's wife smoked marijuana that evening while his daughter played outside. Aaron drank a glass of the Chablis the psychiatrist's wife kept for him at the back of her refrigerator. Aaron and the psychiatrist's wife played three-handed piano and sang arias from *Tosca*. Then the four of them sat and watched the end of *Alice in Wonderland*, beginning with the croquet game. They sat like this on the couch— Aaron, the psychiatrist's wife, the psychiatrist's adopted daughter, the psychiatrist.

Aaron left early, kissing the psychiatrist's wife on the cheek, shaking hands with the psychiatrist. The psychiatrist's adopted daughter went to bed right after that, kissing her father on the cheek and shaking hands with the psychiatrist's second wife.

The psychiatrist was, as they'd both expected, too tired to make love. He had to get up early the next morning to take the dog and the dog's papers back to the kennel. So the psychiatrist's wife secretly touched what private places were left to her, and the familiar motions turned her good hand into an electric stranger.

Her dreams that night were full of Aaron. He was dressed in white and wore a stethoscope, but he looked small. The two of them got on all fours and made love in wet leaves. Aaron said, "This is doggy do," which made the psychiatrist's wife laugh.

The next morning the psychiatrist suggested to his wife that they might better inhabit separate bedrooms for the duration. He said he needed all the rest he could get, and she was making strange noises in her sleep.

"Was I laughing?" asked the psychiatrist's wife.

"Possibly," he said, "It sounded more like growling."

The psychiatrist's second wife sat across from her husband and watched him butter and eat his cold toast. Then she told him there were times she felt like having an affair with Aaron. The psychiatrist stared at his second wife with something like interest for a moment, then he shrugged and began taking the top off his soft-boiled egg.

The psychiatrist's wife was mad. "Don't you have feelings?" she asked.

The psychiatrist looked at her over his half-empty glass of orange juice.

"Of course I have feelings," he said. "They just haven't been called into play yet."

"I understand you less and less," the psychiatrist's wife told him. "What do you mean, *haven't been called into play yet?*"

"Don't quote me to myself," the psychiatrist responded. "I know what I said. If I don't make sense to you, I apologize. But I'm not sloppy with my feelings the way you are. You said you sometimes feel like having an affair with Aaron. I'd have to know what that meant before I felt something about it."

That's not the way it works," the psychiatrist's wife said. "Feelings come first, before you know what anything means."

"Maybe your feelings come first, but some of us— I, for example— happen to belong to the cognitive school of thought. I can give you an article to read, if you'd like."

"Thanks, but no thanks," said the psychiatrist's wife, feeling idiotic, and betrayed. "I'll be too busy having an affair."

Early that evening, she told the psychiatrist she and Aaron were going out for a late supper, and said not to wait up for her.

The psychiatrist looked at her with unfathomable eyes. "What romance did that come from?" he asked. "Have I ever waited up for you?"

The psychiatrist's wife took special care with her appearance that night. She and Aaron went to Gratzi's for a splurge. After the main course, she held his hand under the table. "I want you to make love to me," she said.

Aaron gripped her hand more tightly. "Oh, god," he said. "If only that were possible."

"But it is possible. That's what I'm trying to tell you."

Aaron turned pale. "You don't know what you're saying... You're married. You have a daughter."

"I don't have a daughter, he does." The psychiatrist's wife could tell from Aaron's face that her voice was too loud, but she didn't care. "She's his daughter, not mine."

Aaron's look went moist and blurry at the edges. The psychiatrist's wife felt sick. "That's what this is about, isn't it?" he said, trying to keep her from withdrawing her hand. "You want to have children."

"I don't think so," she said. Then, "Maybe it is. How do I know?"

Aaron smiled. "I'll never forget tonight," he said softly.

"What do you mean?" asked the psychiatrist's wife. She wanted to scream. She wanted to slap him. She was adrift on wave after wave of exhaustion, panic, confusion. A message in a bottle with no shore in sight. "I don't get it. What is there not to forget?"

Aaron's smile never faltered. "I finally realize what I need to do," he said. "You wouldn't be the woman I love if you didn't want children, a family. But I stand in the way of all that. I'm an obstacle between you and the future you deserve." She wanted to strangle him. "You've seen this coming all along, haven't you?" he asked.

"Possibly," the psychiatrist's wife said. She shrugged and pulled out the psychiatrist's American Express card.

A year later, she saw Aaron at a party. He was married, and she was divorced. His wife was at home and pregnant, Aaron said. They had a house and a dog named *"Max."*

He didn't say what kind of dog it was. She didn't ask.

Aaron didn't look intense any more. He looked, instead, devoted, dedicated, devout. He asked how she felt about being divorced. "I don't know yet," she told him. "I haven't figured out what it means."

"Did you get to keep the house?" he asked. To someone else it would have sounded like an afterthought, but she knew better.

"No," she said.

"That's a shame," he told her.

"Maybe not," she said. "He and his third wife probably like it fine—especially now, with all the tulips coming up." She gave him the smile of the bright and beleaguered. Aaron was clearly baffled. He made some excuse and went to talk to someone else. She left the party right after that.

She had no husband, no child, no lover. She didn't know what anything meant. But Fa and Annie would be there when she opened the apartment door. They would crowd around her expectantly, tails wagging, needing to be walked and fed.

The psychiatrist's ex-wife drove home humming "Yes, we have no bananas," and beating time with her good hand on the steering wheel whenever she had to stop for a light.

Hardball

Photo by Danna Byrom

Susan Bright

Which came first?
The metaphor, or the game?

Cosmic Rabbit

Bunny sat on
the edge of the planet
an entire winter
waiting
for the moon
to hatch.

Bunny celebrated Spring.
She decorated eggs.
She didn't understand the symbol.

But she knew
there was a rabbit
in the moon.

She liked the moon.
She liked the way it disappeared.

Photo by Daryl Bright Andrews

Find Holiness. Invent mythical characters.
Close your eyes and look sideways at something
spectacular—Niagara Falls, a mountain covered with
mist or snow, rain falling through the faces in trees.
Find the mythical character playing there. Sometimes
it will be a trickster. Believe it, long enough for the
poem to emerge.

169

Mother Electric

Our Lady of the Mist leaps three hundred feet up—
from a wide snake curve on the Niagara River, thundering
into generators that power the northeastern quarter of a continent.
The Goddess of Electricity leaps out of her own, stone, luxurious,
and cold, tourmaline bone throat.

We see the fog skirt first,
then a translucent waist, mist shoulders,
arms reaching up to dance, cloud face smiling like a full moon
until Northwind blows her out to Nightfall and she leaps up—
again from gravel tumbling itself to a cold shine.
Clear water heart in frost clouds rises too, to kiss our faces,
passionate in rainlight—
and mist is drifting from her finger tips.
She is leaping off a rift in the continent.
She is ripe with exultant falling.

I want to be this goddess,
am drawn into the leap—
pulled into her cold, wet force.

Our Lady of the Mist can tell you about pressure—
cobalt eyes, cloud feet that hold boulders, whitewater, rapids.
She churns essence out to city lights, hotels, traffic.
Tourists in yellow plastic ponchos scurry through wet passages
beneath her skirts, passionate, with flash cameras that record
her advent, catch the essence of her fall, a fall that hot-wires
New York City, Boston, New Hampshire, Montreal, Baltimore, D.C.
Lovers flock to touch the grace of her wet, translucent splash
that never stops pressing against the spin of the earth.

Our Lady of the Mist, Mother Electric, whose emerald velvet gown
leaps out of stone and water at the base of Niagara Falls,
occasionally, because she can, shows herself to us—
because we are slow-witted and don't understand power.

Axe Man

He waited for the ice to melt, for skiers to find him
in a high glacial field in the Italian Alps, fell asleep, berries
and mushrooms in his pockets, waited for us to radio-carbon-date
his bones back to a time before language was written,
except in scratches on cave walls or skin.
A small man, who carried a copper axe that hadn't been invented
yet, he had dark hair, tattoos on his back in sets of fours and fives,
wore shoes woven from grain that grows above 11,000 feet.
Who was this Axe Man anthropologists and three governments
are fighting over hard enough to mutilate 5000-year-old cartiledge?
Did children, parents, friends turn their eyes to the mountains—
imagine him in changing shadows, in flights of birds,
in wind moving through trees? Were there stories of a man
whose shining axe caught light, like mountain lakes
in rough crusts of green? Did mothers warn ill-mannered children,
The Axe Man will get you if you play too far from the fire?
If he had lived to bring the axe back to the valley,
would we be walking among stars now? Or extinct?
Has his DNA snaked to everyone on earth?
Is he the black man with a bald head and dashiki waiting
at the Houston airport? Is he teenagers playing poker,
waiting for a plane to London? Is he the Guatemalan mother
who shouts when everyone else is speaking?
Is the lawyer carrying a cellular phone to the lavatory
on Delta Flight 1164 part of his invention?
Do I carry atoms of a man who died on a glacier in the Italian Alps
near Germany and France, before Germany and France existed?
Did the gene of invention travel through time like a particle shot
into an atom smasher—divide, weave, split, re-group, end up here?
At the Houston airport? In the sky above Lake Mead?
Maybe he just found the axe? Maybe he stole it. Was he Vulcan?
Was the goddess he worshipped a fat Mother Earth?
Did he follow her into musk caverns, until sunlight hit
a vein of metal? Did he plant in our dreams, deeply entwined
in ancestral memory, the outrage of invention?

Wild Pitch

The comet passes close to earth tonight, slips almost
through lunar eclipse, but we will not be fertilized,
will not anguish to dust or turn to finer creatures
with sharp teeth for tearing meat— and heavy bones.

Vegetation will hold its own tonight.
There won't be a collision, oceans won't turn to deserts.
Ice caps won't move to the equator.
Our center will not become our rim. The comet is just
a fuzzy, yellow presence in the northern sky, tail-wiggling
across our window to the universe, which could be anything.
It will pierce something, sometime, but not us, not tonight.

The Firebird, whose heat we cannot imagine,
will be less hot than we are looking up at city lights
beneath a full moon—

Jesse leading off to third,
the pitcher faking a pick-off—

by this small comet that passes close enough for us to see—
a wild pitch, yellow star fuzz.
Someone is going to have a broken jaw.

But we will not be pierced tonight, are lucky tonight.
Our sun won't be obscured. We will not vanish
beneath layers of silt or petrify as pieces of us are replaced
by flint. Tonight somebody's safe.

And the ancient ball game we have created won't be called tonight
by this wild pitch with its flirting journey to the great egg of space.
We'll play on tonight without a clue to the size or form,
meaning, origin or function of the game.

Mother Baseball

Denise knows everything about baseball— team scores, statistics, classic plays, history, the names of all the players. She's a major fan of the Texas Rangers, gets front row seats for all the boys on the little league team, takes them for pictures with José Canseco. She even knows his parents, has pictures of the whole family in her baseball museum, which is most of the living room of her duplex apartment. Denise packs a major league picnic for our games— frozen Sprite, potato chips with ranch dressing, strawberries as big as your fist. She makes banner signs in our team colors, turquoise and black, hangs them from the bullpen fence with shower curtain hooks. Denise explains the plays to me because I don't know anything about baseball. I tell her I come just to make her look good. She looks great, five feet tall, three hundred pounds, caramel skin and a wide Hopi smile. Her grandmother is a medicine woman in Acoma. Her husband, who is not a Hopi, calls Denise *the Indian*. He says she's magic. Denise says her family makes pots. John says her Kachina dolls are incredible. Denise had to go to jury duty last week. She says, *They always pick me*. I say I'd choose her too. Her husband says she should tell them she's Native American and hates white people. Denise says, *Then I'd have to hate my husband and my children*. John asks her why Frank Waters said Hopi Indians were golf fanatics. She doesn't know. She says her mother knows everything about golf. She likes baseball. I call her Mother Baseball. She says the umpire is calling our strikes *balls*. The stands fill up with mothers and fathers, grandparents, aunts, uncles and babies. Our team has great babies and parents that follow them around, clearing a path, parents that hold them in their arms until they go to sleep under baseball lights, where wild parrots live. I watch the children and their parents. Denise watches the game.

Double Suicide

Bases are loaded.
Emiliano, who we call *Stretch,* is on third, and takes
a long lead home. Hank jazzes off second
and the pitcher tries to pick him off—
twice.

Each time Hank, all six-foot-tall, two hundred-forty-pounds
of him, slides back, feet first until he looks like a stucco wall
from the behind—
turquoise shirt on front, sand shirt on the back.

And then it gets crazy—
with Emiliano hanging in the zone between third and home,
Hank sneaks off to third. The batter, a young kid,
looks at them like they're idiots—
and even I know you can't have two guys on third—
Emiliano hanging like turquoise laundry in the wind.

So the pitcher goes for Hank again, throws to second base—
but the second baseman misses the catch
(which almost always happens in South Austin Little League)
allowing Hank and Emiliano to make home plate—
second baseman chasing Hank, the catcher trying to run down
Emiliano, who we call *Stretch.*
Then they're all jumping up and down. *Man, it went just like*
we practiced Man! The pitcher just stood there
glaring at me, Man. I'm just jazzing around on third.
I can't believe that guy missed the ball!
Just like that! Man, I can't believe it worked!

Jesus Poem

Jesus is sitting in a white Chevy van
tonight, silent and dejected,
because things aren't going well.
He took over pitching in the forth inning
and the game fell apart.
All the parents say, *It is OK,*
Jesús played a good game,
and he did. The whole team did—
coming from behind to win
against a team of kids twice their size—
rich kids from across the river
with bad manners.

I want to tell him, *It's never*
just one thing. Take a name, for instance, Jesus,
for instance. It could be God, or just a kid
waiting in the coach's van, a kid we call Chuy,
saying *Come on Chuy, You can do it.*
And he can.

And other times we call him Jesse,
a fifteen-year-old boy with three names,
sad tonight. But he'll be back tomorrow
or the next day, and he'll win,
or practice till he does.

But tonight, beneath the slightest sliver
of a moon, face-up like a bowl,
Jesus is sitting, silent and dejected
in the coach's van— with the equipment.

Shoot Your Television

Yesterday, a man in a dark suit walked up our driveway. John said—
Stop right there. Whatever you're selling, I don't want it. The man
showed us an FBI card. I was thinking of the Federal Building in
Oklahoma City, seven hundred people injured, eighty people dead
because someone hated the government. I was thinking about the
Michigan Militia, men making bombs because they're afraid the
Government will invade their church. I was thinking about the way
I classify the FBI along with the CIA in a bludgeoning pig category.
The FBI man had a list of calls made to us. I was thinking about
attacks on feminists, environmentalists, about children in day care
at the Federal Building in Oklahoma city, how long it took to get
child care for federal employees. Finally, everything in the same
building, all together for the maniac to blow up. I was thinking
about Social Security workers, an entire department crushed, body
bags, a woman's leg being cut off with a pocket knife. I was thinking
how the maniac becomes dangerous. I was thinking about the
Catholic Archbishop who told mourners that God's will was good. I
was thinking about Job, how out of the deepest agony and pain he
screamed, *Why?* I was thinking about Billy Graham, old, wind-worn,
wise, saying Jesus on the cross asked the same question—and then
Billy Graham paused, because he is an orator—until everyone felt
the outrage of *Why?* in their own heart, and then he said, *To make
the world better.* I was thinking how dangerous it is to believe atrocity
makes the world better, how we have to rise up against the maniac. I
wanted to ask mothers, fathers, sons, brothers, sisters if they would
rather have the *warm arms of God around them*—or their families
back, alive, playing in sunlight, snuggling in bed. I was thinking
about soft beige teddy bears people held in place of their own living
children, about red roses wilting as mourners waved them in the air.
I was thinking about God and grief, about atrocity and the Michigan
Militia. We couldn't stop crying, even the President was crying. I
was thinking about how another president commanded Desert
Storm, which resulted in the death of 150,000 children. There was
an FBI agent standing in my driveway. My son wanted to see his gun.

Creeps

Billy Bob says he had no idea
Huey was a creep.
He knew so much about music
and was fun to play with—
mixed it up with the big boys.
Who cared he blew coke?
Who knew he was abusing
children,
dozens of them.

Billy Bob says it makes him
feel stupid
being conned
for twenty-five years
by a creep—
Huey was the source
of so much
of what he wrote about.

Billy Bob says
it almost ruins the music
for him.

Creeps—
the problem with them
is they only talk
to each other.

Even then
they don't hear
anything important.

Out of the Park

State police are transporting
a man to Federal Prison,
so I have to trade for
a safer seat on the airplane.

He is a dark-skinned man.
I see the handcuffs first,
then liquid brown eyes,
an engaging smile.

He's lovable, not frightening,
looks less violent
than the guards who press
both sides against
him so he can't attack
me passing.

I see chains
but he looks like a sitcom
character, this man
who is going
to one of the prisons
we build instead of schools.

He is some woman's son,
for whom, it's now too late.

We watched him grow up.
He played first base, hit one out of the park,
shot the umpire, failed Algebra, twice,
carried contraband from Mexico—
chains on the hands, chains on the feet
of another mother's son.

Strike Zone

If, for example,
you aim at me,
wind up
and throw—
at the right
height
and speed—
and
I'm paying
attention
and functioning
at all—
you're going
to get
smashed.

A hardball,
well thrown
could get hit
out of the ball park
on a good day,
if I'm
paying attention
that is—

Otherwise
I might walk,
steal a base,
slide home.

Home is where I live.
A hard ball
into that strike zone
is very likely
to get smashed.

Mother Coach

My son was a great batter until Denise's son
got hit with a hard ball in the head.

His eye swelled up.
Our pitcher hit the other pitcher in the shoulder
with a fast ball, shying around like it was a mistake.

After that, a lot of the kids were out of synch.
We took them to the batting cages where they hit
ball after ball, but on the field they flinched.

So one day at a family meeting
I stood up, turned into a performer
and recited a poem.

That was performance, I said, This—is just Mom.
I wanted you to see the difference.
When you're in the batting box, you're performing.
You're in charge. Problems don't exist.
You take over.
Later, you're just yourself again.

My son, who listens quickly, said,
Let me see if I got this right.
You want me to step into the batting box,
take a deep breath, swing a few times—
and then read a poem?

Jail for Kids

Sometimes when we play at Lambert Field,
next to the minimum security prison—
a parent leaving the jail
will stop by the game to tell her story—
how her son was caught stealing beer
from a 7-11, how he missed a court appearance,
stole a VCR, sold it to buy drugs,
how someone threw him through a wall,
how he quit school, again, totaled a car, again—
how she has to pay a thousand dollars bail,
and post another thousand to get him out,
how she'd gladly pay it to a hospital, or rehab center
but not to jail, not again.

Sometimes there really is a wall
with one thing inside and something else
on the side the wall can not contain.

But it's our children on both sides,
the ones shouting,
Hey/ Little/ Blue/ Come on/Come on/Just get on/Hey—
Just get on/Hey/Come on/ Come on/Just get on/Hey—

and the ones shouting
I don't have a fucking problem!
I don't need your goddamn help!

They are all our children.

Sex With Aliens

A Harvard psychologist has written a best-selling book,
but the university is upset. It is a mainstream hit, slick marketing.
The author has appeared on television, answering a million
questions about people who have been abducted
by diminutive, large-eyed, gray-colored creatures from space,
who have forced them to have sex. Sex with aliens is not
an academic subject. Harvard is investigating his methodology.
Was there, for example, a control group—people,
who have been abducted by aliens but not forced to have sex?
Were his clients examined by an impartial observer?
What makes a thing academic? If A *equals* B—
(What does it mean? A *equals* B?)
If a phenomenon exists, shouldn't scientists be free to study it?
The author has raised the issue of Academic Freedom.
It's hard for a great university to believe in anything non-verifiable,
unless it's God. Mary had sex with aliens, that's what she said,
and Harvard was founded on that premise.
First person testimony is solid verification,
at least in Social Science, which is an oxymoron.
The Academy studies American Electoral Politics,
Polynesian Puberty Rites, Biblical History, Military Intelligence—
even the Rectal Temperature of Hibernating Bears.
Why not sex with aliens? People ought to *know* if they've had sex
or not, after they get the hang of it. But what's verifiable to you,
or me, may not be verifiable at Harvard where scientists
are expected to play hardball, create hard science, with hard
evidence—but apparently not about aliens with hard sexual parts.

Rudy Dollar

worked for the State Insurance Board for thirty years
and retired and bought a Mexican Chihuahua
to keep her company in her old age.

Rudy Dollar named her dog Miss Peso, who
was smaller than a small cat, meaner than a lion.

They lived on Therapy Street where everyone,
except Miss Dollar and Miss Peso, was either crazy
or a therapist, except for the vet, who was rich.

Rudy Dollar made coats for Miss Peso,
got an umbrella that folded out of the bottom
of a long pole so Miss Peso didn't have
to get wet in the rain.

They walked up and down Therapy Street every morning
and afternoon for twenty years, until Miss Peso died
after which the neighbors didn't see much of Rudy Dollar.

There were high class crazy people on Therapy Street,
and every kind of shrink. Once a year they traded garbage—
rusty fireplace grates, old tables, and metal bunk beds
with one bunk defunct.

At random intervals maniacal teenagers ran up and down
Therapy Street smashing Volvo windowshields
with baseball bats.

That didn't happen
until after Miss Peso died.

Swimming the English Channel

I am woman.
I was born in a Victorian house which I, in turn,
became. By the time I figured it out,
I had already turned into a hotel.

The hotel I am is sometimes alongside an ocean.
City lights behind the hotel I am are galaxies.
In the garage of the hotel, I am apprehended by
family members who want me to behave; I cannot.
Upstairs, someone breaks down the door to one
of my rooms, stretches out on a sofa, and laughs.

I am trying to imagine one life.

I slide backwards, back into a house; this one is modern.
Venetian blinds blind me. I lift them, an ocean
has moved into the front yard. What a view.

Standing on a thin strip of sand outside the house
I am, I see ships racing toward shore, grounding,
running into each other, running into me.

Under a small arch of blue light ships surface and
dive like whales. I stand wide-eyed and search.

Behind me is an enormous dam. It is overflowing;
blue splashes dangerously down.

For shelter, I go back inside.

There is a grizzly bear in the kitchen. Bars
set up half-heartedly do not particularly contain it.
Leaving is necessary.

I become a pilgrim. In the wilderness is bedlam.

Masses wander through forests going to judgment,
nuclear holocaust, for instance.

I quit being a pilgrim telling myself,
whatever is gnawing at my heart, pulling me forward
from inside and outside, whatever it is—it can't be that bad.

I am a woman trying to imagine a path into the future—
Men—are going there too.

I turn into an automobile. The mechanical parts are scrambled.
The steering wheel is in the back seat.
I am a van. Doors fall open, slide closed, headlights
are blunt against darkness.

Downhill is a man in a neon fluorescent dome.
I get my driving parts together and go;
but there is a red light, so I stop.
The man steps out of dream and tells me he is trying
to make the light work. I fall in love.

Waves splash every place. I drive.
Streets stretch flat along the ground, but the landscape
keeps changing. One street becomes all streets.
I am all women loving all men. That makes me a theater.

I have seven stories and flying drops.
My 4th floor is outdoors, wide open, like New Mexico,
a brown prairie.

It is surprising
to start out inside, then suddenly, be outdoors—
exposed.

In the rest of the theater I am, backdrops fly up
and down at slant angles.
On the 2nd floor is an art exhibition from the 21st Century.
Gigantic white tea cups and saucers are set out on a plain stage.
They are a joke.

In the basement of the theater I am, an old man
turns a wheel that controls my sets.

I am a woman
shouting
at the 21st Century.

I did not intend to be a theater.
I do not like the man in the basement who controls me.
I do not want to be a house, a hotel, a car.
I do not like being exposed.

I am amazed by the waves that are flooding my body and spirit.
I do not like the grizzly bear in my kitchen.
There is chaos in the forest, a dam is spilling over behind me.
Ships leap out of the water at me, and the end of the world
is a distinct possibility.

I turn into a boat.
The waves are gigantic, the boat is just a few slats,
air rushes through spaces between them. An old sailor
says he knows something important but to forget it.

I float on layers and layers of water like grass, billowing
in green light. I am shouting.

I am shouting!
I am full to the teeth
with ideas that don't work, with containers that don't
hold water, and water is everyplace.

I turn into a construction site. Boards and slats lean
against plaster walls. Shingles hinge themselves to light fixtures.
White tubes stick out of ceiling beams.
The attic is the only place I like.

It is a loft. You can see out.
You can see stars through holes in the roof.

I expand.
I start to fly, search.
Searching, I am the air.

I am woman flying—
I lean into the wind of the universe,
admit it.

I accelerate, become a path. There are signs.
They point to a ladder. It is erratic, pegs legs swing wide,
it sways into starlight. It ought to work, but it doesn't.
I look at it and say, *No way I'm being that damn ladder
again!*

I turn into
a gate.
Outside the sun shines.

Pavement stretches ahead, through and behind me.
I drive a real car, the one I make payments on, into
the countryside. I pass a dancing tree.

A souped-up Volkswagen passes me going fast. The driver
holds up a sideways oval sign on a stick. It is red.
It says,
        S M I L E,

so I do.

I laugh at these changes,
at this awkward metamorphosis, this disintegrated integration,
these torn apart forms, this confusion of scaffolding.

I am Changing Woman, conjuring a future to turn into—
men—are conjuring, too.
I flow through structures too dull for me into others so vast
I am lost.

I am like you. My soul unpeels slowly, folding in, reaching
out, in to self, out to you.

You trust me the way you have to trust yourself.
I can slip into your imagination or into your arms.
We flow through each other like the tide of a century turning.

It turns hard, but it turns.
It flows rough in long waves; you can't stop it.

Myth of Proportion

And snakes are only rivers, sealed up rivers that slide along,
self-contained, like truth, where everything is red clay,
or desert. And moisture exposed to air will vanish
into hot light or be sucked up by grain the way
the Colorado River never makes it to the sea
because of Hoover Dam—named after the man
Very-Old-Grandmother said was the dumbest person
who ever lived, because he ordered farmers to gas torch
cattle, not for supper, but to drive up the price of grain,
during the Depression, when people were starving.
And the red canyons that grew into Lake Mead gleam
like Depression glass when you look down from clouds.
And arroyos feather out like crystals in time
the way large and small reverse themselves. And Sky
is full of holes that are invisible but shake up everything
that passes through them. And time is an invention
that keeps everything from happening at once.
And reality is the Snake that ate a river.
And we are the Snake.

About the Artists

Ann Williamson lives in Michigan with her husband. She is part of the Writers in the Schools program there, received a Creative Artist Grant from the Michigan Council for the Arts in 1986, won the Abbie M. Copps Award from Olivet College in 1991, and tied for first place in the Poet Hunt Contest from Schoolcraft College in 1993. She has two books: **Wild Rumors,** from Lake Shore Publishing, and **Too Hot, Too Cold, Just Right,** from Plain View Press in 1995.

Naomi Louisa Mountjoy Long received a degree from the Sydney Kindergarten Training College. Her teaching experience spans two continents and four decades, specializing in pre-school training, youth work and developing residential camps. She was directly involved in the Civil Rights Movement by setting up Head Start centers in rural Mississippi. Currently, she works at Upland Hills School in Michigan, an alternative educational community where she has been teaching for more than fifteen years. Many of her essays have appeared in *Eco-Logic*, a newsletter from the Upland Hills Awareness Center. Her interests include day walks, writing and wood carving.

Carol Cullar is editor of *The Maverick Press* and the *Southwest Poets' Series*. Her poetry collection, **Pagan Heart,** was one of five Honorable Mentions in the Salmon Run Press National Poetry Book Award for 1995. **Inexplicable Burnings** won the Press of the Guadalupe 1992 Chapbook Contest. Carol has had work accepted for publication or recently published by *The New York Quarterly, Kansas Quarterly, Negative Capability, Voices West, The MacGuffin, Parnassus Literary Review, Pinyon Poetry, Frontiers: A Journal of Women Studies, RE:AL, Fireweed: A Feminist Quarterly* (Canada), *Zuzu's Petals Review, New Texas '95, Borderlands, et alteros.* She is the author of *Haiku, This Hunger,* and *Life & Death, Mostly.* A visual artist and licensed pilot, mother of two and grandmother of one, Carol lives on the fringes of the Chihuahua Desert near the banks of the Rio Grande outside Eagle Pass, Texas.

Margo LaGattuta is a poet with four published books: **Embracing the Fall** (Plain View Press), **The Dream Givers** (Lake Shore Publishing), **Noedgelines** (Earhart Press) and **Diversion Road** (State Street Press). Her poems and essays have appeared in *The Bridge, Passages North, Yankee, Cincinnati Poetry Review, The MacGuffin, The Little Magazine, Negative Capability, The New Laurel Review, The Sun PhonomeNews,* and others. Among her national awards are The Midwest Poetry Prize and the Founder's Award of the National Federation of State Poetry Societies. An editor for Plain View Press, she has an MFA from Vermont College, teaches writing at Oakland Community College and through her business, Inventing the Invisible, she hosts a weekly radio program in Bloomfield Hills, Michigan, called *Art in the Air*.

Patricia Alice Albrecht received her BFA in Theatre from Wayne State University. She's spent the last 18 years in Los Angeles doing theatre, t.v., film, radio and voice work for animation as well as visual art. Her work has appeared in various small presses, most recently, *Rattle* and *360 Degrees, Art and Literary Review*. The Noisy River Publishing Colony marks the transition as she leaves a home in Malibu to live with her husband and son in Nashville.

Shanda Hansma Blue is a non-traditional student in the Lee Honors College of Western Michigan University, finishing her BA with majors in English and Women's Studies, and a minor in Psychology. She will begin work on an MFA in English/Writing in 1997. Shanda has been published in *The Louisville Review*, *The Southern Indiana Review*, *The Flying Island*, and other regional publications. In her previous life, she was a mom, an elected town council member, an appointed member of the board of trustees of Syracuse Public Library and a trustee of Lakeland Community Services, a community-owned and operated daycare center

Lyn Coffin has two books of poetry: **The Poetry of Wickedness,** (Ithaca House) and **Human Trappings** (Abattoir Editions). She has published translations from German, Russian and Czech: **The Poetry of Anna Akhmatova** (W. W. Norton), Orten's *Elegies* and Seifert's *The Plague Column* (CVU Press). **Elegies** won first prize in an International Poetry Review Competition, and **The Plague Column** was read by the committee that granted Seifert his Nobel Prize. Lyn's poetry and fiction have been widely published. *"Falling Off the Scaffold"* was in **Best American Short Stories,** edited by Joyce Carol Oates. Her plays have been performed at many theaters, including the Attic Theatre in Detroit. Lyn is an editor of **The Michigan Quarterly Review.** She graduated Phi Beta Kappa from the University of Michigan, winning Hopwood Awards in every category and an Academy of American Poets Prize. She is currently a Ph.D. candidate.

Susan Bright is author of fourteen books of poetry, three of which (**Far Side of the Word, Tirades and Evidence of Grace** and **House of the Mother)** have been recipients of Austin Book Awards. She is the editor of Plain View Press, which for the twenty-one years between 1975 and 1996 has published one-hundred-and-twenty books. Her work as a poet, publisher, activist and educator has taken her all over the country. In

Texas she has received a proclamation from the Senate honoring her literary and community work and in Austin she received the Woman of the Year Award in 1990 from the Women's Political Caucus *"in recognition of outstanding leadership and initiative in helping to improve the quality of life for women and their families in Austin and Travis County."* She is editor of *"Women's Way,"* a feminist newspaper, and coordinator of the Women's Way Festival, which has been held in Austin to celebrate Women's History Month every year since 1986.

Trained as an architect and photographer, **Marty Burnett** combines both passions into the colorful, emotion-provoking collection, *"The High Road Series."* *"The Laced Window"* (front cover) and *"Turquoise Door"* (back cover) are two of more than forty photographs in this collection. *"In our fast-paced, changing world, we need symbols that are a reminder of the timeless, ongoing world of the spirit. Actually, our day-to-day lives are filled with such symbols. What we must learn is to slow our pace and open our awareness to their existence in order to utilize these symbols for our spiritual illumination. For most of my life, I have been drawn to structural openings as a spiritual passageway."* These photographs are available as notecards or signed, limited editions from Green River Photography, Austin, TX.

Bruce Michael Miller has toured the world as lead guitarist for Laura Branigan and sung with Paul McCartney and Kenny Loggins. Performance has led him to song writing which he now pursues in Nashville. Photography is one of several art media in which he works.

Daryl Bright Andrews is the son of Susan Bright and John C. Andrews. He has been a founding class member of two alternative schools, has worked as a bike mechanic, salesperson and carpenter's helper. His interests are baseball, swimming, diving and art.

Windows to the Soul

Squeal - Have a baby. Tell the truth about it. Lie about it. Give yourself permission to reinvent fact and truth whenever possible. (Albrecht) (See Albrecht, *"I Just Thought It Was Menopause."*)

Histrionics - Choose two current event personalities or historical figures and engage them in a conversation. Find out how your voice emerges through them and learn why their position is so sacred to them. (Albrecht)

Shivers - Tell five rules about everyday things that you had as a child. In *"Baby Birds"* the child licks the piece of candy and puts it back in the serving dish. I shivered when I wrote that. Write a mini story about each rule on your list. (Williamson)

Magic Glyphs - The petroglyphs reminded me of a prompt I invented for first and second graders. I made up a sheet of symbols and a few words and they wrote (told) the story they found there. (Williamson)

Author Sandwich - Take two radically different authors and try to combine their styles or themes in a single poem. (Coffin)

Incognito - Go some place you've never been and be a fly-on-the-wall. Write down whatever you're inspired by. Examples: A divey bar at 10:00 a.m., a church you've never been in, a political meeting, anyplace you will be a minority. (Coffin) (See LaGattuta, *"Stopping for a Bite."*)

Puzzled - When suffering from writer's block, I sometimes write a poem using the clues in the New York Times crossword puzzle. I suggest starting at the end and working backward. (Coffin)

Fortune Smiles - In a group it's fun to have each member arrive at the writing session with a list that is not labled or identified until after the poems (each person writing from someone else's list) are written. Use *Tarot* card names (insist that every word be used), plant classifications, body parts, etc. An almanac or encyclopedia could serve as a source. (Cullar)

Myth Mutation - Take an ancient myth from a culture other than your own and rewrite it in contemporary terms, or take a minor character or a villian and make a new myth with a new heroine or hero. (Cullar) (See Cullar, *"Fire, Rain and the Need to Act"* or *"The Serpent Asks, 'Why Not?'"*)

Get Personal - Have a dialogue with your inner child, or your inner male or inner female (opposite sex). Tell her/him what you have not told anyone else. (Cullar) (See Blue, *"Breathe through your nose"* or *"Spanish Market."*)

Source List - Make a list of your favorite words, then trade with a friend. Try writing from a new vocabulary. (Cullar) (See Cullar, *"Border Crossing."*)

Word Up - Pick an evocative word from the dictionary, familiar or unfamiliar. Let your mind wander freely to all the associations triggered by that word, write your thoughts. (Cullar) (See Cullar, *"The Sound of Gravid."*)

Epiphanies—Write a poem about a frightening (or exhilarating) experience you've had. Give specific details. Now turn that experience into a metaphor for something else. (LaGattuta) (See LaGattuta, "Bats" poem.)

Tasks—Write about an ordinary household chore (like folding towels, mowing the lawn, etc.). Find a way to exaggerate, lie, or use surrealism to make a point. Let humor and irony be your guide. (LaGattuta) (See LaGattuta, "Linen" poem.)

Copy Change— Choose a favorite free verse poem by another writer. Make a list of details about its form and content, its strategies. For example the poem might use all present tense verbs, or begin (or end) with a question, or pile up a list of leaping images—then make an ironic closure, etc. Now construct an original poem about a different subject but use the same strategies. (LaGattuta)

Noun Soup —Write a poem that includes the following: 1. a famous person, 2. a food, 3. an article of clothing, 4. a restaurant, 5. a hotel, 6. another article of clothing, 7. a city or town, 8. a beverage, 9. a game and 10. a family member.(LaGattuta) (See LaGattuta, "Looking for Elvis in Kalamazoo.")

Word Chains —Pick an interesting noun. Brain storm a list of 7 to 9 words from that word. (Let each word make you think of the next word.) Create the list of words perpendicular in the middle of a page. Now snake a poem around that list. Each word has to be somewhere within the line. Each line can be as long or short as you want, but the poem has to fit within the 7 to 9 lines. (LaGattuta)

Fibbing—Invent ten enormous fibs about your life. Make them very specific and very outrageous. Now look over the list and make one or more of them into a poem. Write it in the present tense. (LaGattuta)

Dreams — Keep a record of your dreams when you first remember them in the morning. Choose an unfinished scenario and write a poem that finishes it, or re-write a dream with an ending you like better. (LaGattuta)

Kitchens — On large unlined paper use markers or crayons to draw the first kitchen you remember from your childhood. (Or the first bedroom.) Fill in all the specific details (like Philco refrigerator). When you finish, note images and memories in clusters of language all over the drawing. Now begin a poem with some memories this triggered. Use as many specifics as you can. (LaGattuta) (See Williamson, "What the Universe Looks Like From Earth.")

Shocks—Brain storm as many memories as you can recall from an important and shocking event in history. Where were you when Kennedy died or when the Gulf War started? What was the color of the tablecloth? Who was with you? Write a poem from your notes. (LaGattuta) (See LaGattuta, "Stopping for a Bite" or Bright, "Shoot Your Television.")

Walking in Your Own Shoe—Take off one of your shoes and place it in front of you. Make a brainstorm list of where this shoe has taken you, where it's going, how it fits, etc. Now write a poem from these images. (LaGattuta)

Gossip—Read one of the tabloids (National Enquirer, Star, etc.) and write a poem about one of the most outrageous stories, or make up your own gossip story about a famous person. Pretend to be one of the characters in the story (i.e. a housewife abducted by aliens) and spin a wild invented tale. (LaGattuta) (See Bright, "Sex With Aliens.")

194

Metaphor for the Self—Choose something from nature or from the technological world and speak in its voice for ten minutes while you are also listening to music or sitting someplace where there is background commotion. Once you start writing in the voice of this thing—*"I am the wind, I fall out of the sky, I blow through your ears and make you crazy, I am the wind, etc."* Don't stop writing for any reason. If you run out of things to say—write down numbers, or types of fruit—any category. Then start up again when another related idea appears. (Bright) (See Bright, *"Swimming the English Channel,"* or Long, *"I am a Feather."*)

From the Edge—Write a dream. Paint with magic markers the same dream. Write the dream a second time. Find an image you left out, a detail missed, emphasized, or somehow treated differently. Identify the change in your perception of the dream. Write about whatever it is you found on the "edge" of consciousness. (Bright) (See LaGattuta, *"The Dream Givers."*)

Eavesdrop—Sit someplace where you can hear other people talking. For a half hour write down the exact words you hear—or snippets of what you hear. Change something. Mix it into a poem you've started and set aside. (Bright) (See Bright, *"Double Suicide,"* or *"Jail for Kids,"* or Long, *"Sit Back and They Come"*)

Sorry—Write a letter of apology to someone. (Don't send it necessarily.) Write an answer to your letter of apology from that person. Give yourself a hard time. Create a dialogue between yourself and the other person by turning the exchange from letters to a phone conversation. Create a scene by putting the two people in the same room to "have it out." (Bright) (See Albrecht, *"Happy Happy Birthday Baby,"* or Long, *"I Hear Myself Crying."*)

Forbidden—Make a list of things you would never be able to write about. Write about one of those things every day for a week. (Bright) (See Albrecht, *"Blue Legs."*)

Pissed—Make a list of things that infuriate you. Write about one of those things every day for a week. (Bright) (See, Bright, *"Strike Zone"* or Long, *"I Really Don't Know."*)

Dillusional—Write a dialogue between yourself and an inanimate object—a lamp post, television, a dumpster. Re-write the dialogue from the point of view of the inanimate object. (Bright) (See Williamson, *"An Egg."*)

Sore Spot—Write about something that has been causing you pain until you feel better. This could take time—an hour, a decade. (Bright) (See Williamson, *"November,"* or *"What Will Become of Us All,"* or Coffin, *"The Psychiatrist's Second Wife."*)

Real Life Editing—Examine a situation that turned out badly. Write about the situation. Give it a different ending. (Bright) (See Coffin, *"Point of View Problems."*)

Mining—Look at a prose section in your journal. Underline the essential phrases and words. Rewrite the piece as a poem including only the essence of the journal material. Allow the piece to evolve to coherence, or mystery. Weave into this images or excerpts from earlier or later sections in the journal. See what happens. (Bright)

Mockingbird—Speak in the voice of a relative you remember from a long time ago. Make a list of their "sayings." (Bright) (See Long, *"And What's in the Drawer?"*)

Character—(group exercise) Make up a name. Write it on a piece of paper. Pass the paper to a friend. Have the person write down an age. Pass the paper to another friend who can write down a physical description. Pass the paper around a circle having people add things: the character's goals, the character's best friend, a dream the character had, a problem, something heroic, something ridiculous. Describe the house the character grew up in. Keep adding information until you've created a history. Use the group notes as the basis for a character portrait. (Bright)

Tableau—Create an action, photo-like scene using less than twenty words, one word to a line. Create these from memory, or by looking at art books. Use artists from different periods of time, schools of art, cultures. Create a series of tableau poems. (Bright) (See Long, *"The Lawn Was Still Green."*)

Point of View—Write five sentences about something dramatic you've recently witnessed—jumping a creek, diving into a pool, an auto accident, a child falling down, getting up again. Re-write it from a second point of view. If you began with "he" or "she," try writing it in first person— "I". Then write it from a third (inanimate) point of view, how the water sees the diver, for example. Then write it from the point of view of someone looking down from outer space, or from a helicoptor flying overhead. Write it from as many points of view as you can imagine. (Bright) (See Bright, *"Jail for Kids"* or Coffin, *"Point of View Problems."*)

Journey—Each person in a group of six or more people paints (with markers on large sheets of paper) a dream. Tape the paper dreams to a wall, or a series of windows. Starting anywhere, describe a journey from dream to dream. If, as Carl Jung says, dreams are the windows to the soul—the journey will be a journey through the psyche. Include colors, textures, emotions, archtypes. Allow your journey to be nonsensical, or mold it into something that makes sense. (Bright)

House—Draw, with markers on a large sheet of paper, the floor plan of a house you lived in when you were young. Add as much detail as you can remember—where doors, windows, closets were. Alongside the drawing, make lists. What did each room smell like? Who lived there? Who lived nearby? List friends in the area, teachers at the nearby school, kinds of plants outside, the names of people in the extended family, names of nearby streets. Select details and build them into poems or stories. Write a poem about your closet, or room, or favorite shirt. Write about the living room sofa. Write about your sister's voice. The smells in the basement. (Bright) (See **House of the Mother** by Susan Bright, Plain View Press, 1995 or LaGattuta, *"My Welcome Home Illusion,"* or

Long, "*Recital.*")

Print—What does your poem look like in print? Are the lines long, or short? Is it a prose poem, scattered all over the page, or is it written in a large "0?" Why is it shaped like it is shaped? If you have no idea, create one. Create an idea about why your poems look the way they do. Choose a poem you're not sure how to finish. Make it look a dozen different ways on the page. Pick the best presentation. (Bright)

Blab School—In a group of six or more people give each person something mundane to read. Introduce these reading techniques: 1. Read part of the sentence very loudly (shout), another part very softly(whisper); 2. Read part in a high-pitched voice, part in a low-pitched voice; 3. Read part in a dramatic voice (HELP!); 4. Read part in a lyrical voice (gentle, pretty); 5. Imitate the six o'clock newscaster; 6. Pretend you're reading a fairytale to a small (lucid) child. Everyone read at once, practice over and over each technique. What you're saying—in this exercise— makes no difference, it's *how* you say it. 7. Read fast. Read slow. 8. Find pauses. Flick lights for the goup to start. Flick lights for them to stop. (Bright)

Revision Exercises-Poetry (LaGattuta)

It is always a blow to the ego to have a poem you love rejected by an editor. However, after the initial disappointment, you have three choices: I. Forget it, and never write again; 2. Assume it is just not right for that publisher, but send it elsewhere; 3. Begin the revision process, revise it, then send it out again.

If you choose option I, you're out of the process, and you can count on never getting published. Option 2 might work. Try it and if, after three more tries, the poem is still rejected, you are ready for option 3. This one really works, if you're willing to work hard and study the craft of revision. These are some approaches to revision—not necessarily to be done in this order.

a. Does the poem need expansion? Does it have some wonderful images and beginnings but ideas that are not developed fully enough for the reader to get involved? Make sure you don't leave out something crucial because it doesn't "fit" logically. If it feels connected (associatively), get it in the poem somehow.

b. Does the poem need shrinking? Did you go past a powerful ending and add just one or two more lines to say "Get it?" to the reader? Are there unnecessary opening lines, which you needed to get the poem started, but they're no longer needed to enhance meaning?

c. Is the language lazy or ordinary? Have you used too many cliches or uninteresting nouns and verbs? Are there too many adjectives or adverbs? Remember, in poetry the ideas are much stronger with fewer distractions. Less is more (unless it's not enough!).

d. Notice line breaks. Does the poem read aloud well? Does it sound right if you take a breath where the line breaks? Are there all end-stopped lines, or do you vary them with enjambments? (Breaking the line between an adjective and a noun, for example.) Does the poem sound better written in prose (without selected line breaks)?

e. Are there rewards for the reader? Does the poem grab his/her attention with power right away? Could the parts (lines, stanzas) be rearranged to make the order more interesting, or more logical? Does the ending leave the reader with an epiphany? Or a let down?

f. Look at the voice. Does it talk down to the reader, or make him/her feel dumb or lectured? Remember, if the voice endears itself to the reader, you're ahead!

g. Is the poem universal? Remember, we not only want to tell our story (the reader, unless it's our mother, might not care). We want the reader to find his/her own story in it. Metaphor is a wonderful technique for this.

h. Is the poem sentimental or emotional? Sentiment doesn't move the reader. It usually just moves the writer. The reader needs to feel the emotion —not be told. Often a poem is sentimental if it doesn't deal with enough tension of opposites. Emotions are not just black or white. They're more complex (good can be bad, etc.). Oxymoron works well for this.

i. What is the emotional context of the poem? Do you know something you don't want to tell the reader? Is there some information you could add that would illuminate the meaning somehow?

j. If the poem is in the first person, try it in the second or third person.

k. Are there some logical connective tissues that are needed, or can you remove some—so the mind has to leap from part to part in the poem?

Revision Exercises—Fiction (Bright)

Use these exercises to inform your work and spark your imagination as you work on the second, third, etc. drafts of fiction pieces. Keep multiple versions of your revisions so if you go too far you can retreat to an earlier (better) version. On the other hand, if you stumble into something wonderful, keep it. Don't worry if you stray from your story outline. Worry if you don't.

a. Create a history for each character, separate from the story. Write pages of detailed history. As this history suggests episodes, add them to the story. As it suggests motivation, revise your characters actions so they are consistent with who the person is.

b. Use the Method Acting technique of living with a character so that he or she can grow real. "What would he do if— What would she do if— Fill in the blank. Invent a hundred "if-situations." Decide what your character would do. Use this information to inform the development and revision of your story.

c. Find a passage in which you tell the reader what has occurred but did not "show" the reader how it happened. We call that "collapsing" a story. Expand it. Get characters talking, acting, moving. Turn your narrative passage into a scene.

d. Rewrite a scene from four different points of view. Choose the one that is most effective.

e. Arrive at a point in your story from which you have no idea how to proceed. Take a hot bath, no lights, just a candle or two. Soak. Ask for a dream. Do this several days in a row. From the dream, choose a direction for the story.

f. Talk to yourself. Answer. Begin to do this in the voices of your characters.

g. Take a story that is 80% narrative, or more, and write it in dialogue.

h. Take a story that isn't working and add a character. Weave the new person into every scene. Make it a contentious character if your story is boring. If the story is too intense, add a peacemaker. If everyone is old, add a child. Let the new character revise the story for you.

i. Take a story that isn't working and change gender roles. Turn the male characters into female characters, the female characters into men. Revise speeches and actions to allow for gender differences, but retain the plot, or change it.

j. Make decisions about punctuation for dialog and follow them consistently. Ask a detail-oriented friend to proof read.

k. Check your story for details. If a character has died, don't have them answering the phone in the next scene, unless you are revising to add surreal detail to a story that is too realistic. Less obvious details can also goof up a story. Another good job for the detail-oriented friend.

l. Read your story outloud. Fix the passages that don't work.

m. Write an aesthetic statement in which you define in some way your writing style and the subject matter that informs your work. Compare your statement to your work. Let the work inform the aesthetic statement, and allow the aesthetic statement to inform the work.